GREAT WHITE DEATH

S.J. LARSSON

SEVERED PRESS

HOBART TASMANIA

GREAT WHITE DEATH

Copyright © 2018 by Severed Press

WWW.SEVEREDPRESS.COM

ISBN: 978-1-925840-27-8

PROLOGUE

There is a shark of legends in the waters around Aña Nuevo Island. A great white. He goes by the name Great White Death, and stories of his devastation stretch back as far as 400 years ago. Some say he is 20 feet long. Others say he is 30. Some, even bigger.

Great White Death is said to enjoy killing. Killing anything. His favorite pastime is destruction of his own kind. He kills any other great white that dares enter his territory. Every one of his stories describes his killing, of other sharks, seals, and especially the humans who've attempted to live in the area, as bloody. Very bloody. Great White Death likes to break his prey into pieces, leaving their souls the only things left for him to swallow once his teeth are finished.

He is only seen in storms. Every single tale of Great White Death takes place in a horrific Pacific Ocean sea storm. They say he likes storms because it makes his attacks more terrifying to his victims. Makes sense. After all, he enjoys killing, right? So, of course he'd want to make it as scary as possible. For this shark, it's said the thrill is the only reason he eats. He thrives on his feasts screaming and flailing in horror. Some stories even say he has a smile when he finishes, and that he swallows almost immediately after his food finally stops moving for good.

No two make the same sounds when utterly tortured.

No two make the same sounds when gored by Great White Death.

There are so many legends of him locals know, yet no tale tells of a survivor. No sightings reported. Only the stories passed from sailor to sailor, mother to son to grandson have spread, and they all end in everyone dead, destroyed by the great white's steel-hard teeth. Nobody questions how his existence and his bloody killings could be known, so detailed, with not even a witness to a slaughter ever recorded in a single piece of lore.

His earliest slaughter was in 1641.

It was here, on Aña Nuevo Island. A local tribe held weddings here, and in 1641, a beautiful 16-year-old girl was marrying a 15-year-old boy in a tempest.

It is said the local witch spilled bat blood into the sea. She usually did curses only when paid, but this curse was a personal vendetta, one she knew she'd also suffer the consequences of. The girl's mother had stolen her father from the witch when they, too, had been young, and married on Aña Nuevo Island. Revenge. The bat blood was said to bring Great White Death from his depths like steak brings a dog. The witch knew of such things, and that's how Great White Death was invited to a wedding feast of terror on Aña Nuevo Island in 1641.

People could hardly see each other because of the weather, which was some point of doing such ceremonies on the island during a storm, and there is said to be about 30 of them there. 30 men, women, grandmothers, grandfathers, sons, daughters…a bride and groom…and remember, there were never any survivors.

The thunder was their music, the rainfall their voices, lightning their fireworks.

They had a shark lookout. Aña Nuevo has always had great whites, so they always had at least one shark lookout when near shark-infested waters.

The thing was, the shark lookout never got a chance to give a warning. The witch dropped her bat blood in the sea below his rocky perch.

Great White Death isn't afraid of the land or lack of air.

The shark launched himself at the lookout, mouth eager and wide, full of decrepit yet sharp teeth. The lookout did call out. He wailed, he begged and cried before Great White Death was done, but it during was a noisy part of the ceremony where everyone shouts words of advice to the newlyweds. The witch designed it that way.

Nobody could see more than a few feet in front of them because of the heavy rain. They didn't see the shark lookout's bloody and painful demise.

Once the lookout uttered his last, the shark swallowed him, went under, and then dove, sliding on his belly, up on the beach and right into the wedding, mouth open, eyes rolled back, wearing a slight smile, they say. He scooped up three people in that dive, and immediately began slowly, gently tasting them as they screamed.

Then, everybody saw him. He was enormous, a shark so wicked-looking it had to be from a witch's curse, and everybody knew they were doomed as Great White Death thrashed about, gnawing on bits and parts of people while they wailed. The shark seemed to be able to breathe air. Not even the storm's rain could wash those rocks back clean from the gore of his mess and blood. The sounds of their tormented dying are said to be heard by sailors in storms near the island over the years, phantoms of horror stuck in time…

Chapter One – Day 1

"You're so full of shit, Lex," Oliver said, laughing and shaking his head. "There's no 400-year-old shark here."

Lex tipped his hat up and smiled at Oliver. "That we are positive about."

Diane stood up and chucked her empty beer can at the trash bin. It landed. "Okay, okay. You two aren't allowed to get started." She bent over Lex and kissed him, then stood straight. "It would be nice if Melody doesn't have explain to Oliver that you enjoy getting him pissed for once after beers."

Lex took off his hat and shook his black curls. The humidity made him sweat, Diane saw. "I don't like getting Oliver pissed."

Oliver waved his beer through the air. "She said it, not me."

"Then why do you tell a gore-fest story like that about a shark we're anchored at's island?" She put her hand on her hip.

"Because I like scaring people." He grinned at her. Winked.

She winked back. "Go scare Aaron. He likes your kind of crazy."

"I think I will. Where are you going?" He stood up, steadying himself on the yacht's deck against the rough waters. The storm was coming in, just as they'd hoped.

"Dr. Hammerstein wanted me to help scope out some of the cameras before the storm really picks up."

Melody leaned forward. "You're not supposed to be working. It's time to call it a day. Have another beer."

Diane shook her blonde head. "No time. This is my game. Got to do it right."

Melody pretended to toast an imaginary beer in front of her. Diane cracked up as Melody said, "Take one with ya!"

She paused as she turned to the ladder. Looked over her shoulder at Lex. Scrambled to the cooler, pocketed a can, and then down the ladder she went.

*

As Diane passed the enormous, derelict lighthouse keeper's home from eons ago, she thought about Lex. She'd never gone for the hot type, if you could call it that, and Lex wasn't exactly hot-guy personality type, but yeah. He was hot. Diane giggled to herself. That guy got her so bad that she reverted to thinking her reasonings with ninth grade wording.

They'd anchored at the beach across from the house and the other beach where they'd be studying the sea lions' behavior during summer storm season. Just a five-day trip on the isolated island, but Dr. Hammerstein made it happen—she'd gone to him with her proposal for the study, and he pushed for funding through the school. Stanford took its marine biology school and its students seriously—Dr. Hammerstein especially so—and Diane was granted the funding. The best part was she got to pick her crew. Dr. Hammerstein was a no-brainer.

Lex was, too, even though his area of study was sharks. Still, he was going. Diane couldn't stand to be away from him for a night, much less five days. She'd used his shark specialty as a selling point because there were sharks around Aña Nuevo Island.

Melody, Diane's roommate and best friend, had given her the idea for the proposal to do the study, and she had to be there. She was an expert on aquatic life in the seas outside Northern California, too, which was perfect. Plus, Melody had gotten Diane on track with this particular project—they shared it, in truth.

Aaron was into marine botanicals, which would help, and Lex was happy to find out he was into other botanicals. Who wasn't? Aaron wanted to bring his black lab, Kirby, along. Everybody on the trip was an animal lover, so he was a welcome addition, but Dr. Hammerstein said it was against policy. Diane had an impossible time talking him into leaving Kirby for a week.

Oliver had some kind of massive memory. He could remember everything he'd ever read. Not heard or have seen, just read. Invaluable resource on a research trip where they'd have no access to the Internet. Diane could tell Lex hated him, and she got it. Oliver talked a big game, and Lex found it annoying. So, he egged it on until Oliver was fighting just to fight. Lex told her that's why he did it—he was trying to show the guy what it's like to talk to himself.

Bunny was along for tech work, but this was also her field. Melody liked to say Bunny was into the production side of marine biology. Diane didn't know her too well, but that wasn't because she never saw her. Bunny was shy, or so it seemed to Diane. She was a watcher. She would also be notating the trip.

Chas was the main tech worker. He was in his last year of graduate studies. Diane thought he was a smart one, quick. He loved politics, but respected that not everybody loved politics. She was grateful for that. Politics right then were an explosive subject. She liked to keep the peace.

Then there was Joseph. He had been her lab partner for two years in marine mammal studies. They'd dissected god knows how many sea creatures and critters, something they both found fascinating. They related on how they could talk about it with each other and not sound like weirdo creeps.

Lex didn't like that.

Of course, it was still a new relationship, just six months in, but they'd known each other since undergrad. Hell, they'd *all* known each other since undergrad. Diane had even had a class with Chas when she was a senior. Lex hadn't shown any other horrible qualities than a little jealousy over her and Joseph talking about sea guts. Diane would take it, because she knew from personal experience that there was worse, a lot worse, than jealousy at what Diane admitted to herself bordered on flirting.

It never meant anything, though. Not to Joseph, either. Diane could tell.

Lex was the one for her, always had been.

"There you are. How was your beer?" Dr. Hammerstein called out to her from the beach. It was a little inlet with a rocky beach, and sea lions were everywhere. "Be careful. Come around to the sea line and make sure those camera poles are secure, will ya? Triple check." He bent back over a hole he was digging. She wondered what that was for, and then started watching the sea lions getting restless from people being around them, too close.

"We have to hurry, Dr. Hammerstein," she said. "I'll check all the perimeter cameras on this side. You get the others and we'll pack it up for the night." She smiled at him.

"You're right. What the hell is this irrigation hole going to do? I'm not going to get consistent anything in the storm to come." He wiped his forehead and flipped the shovel over his shoulder. "Keeping busy to keep busy, I suppose."

"It's okay. You're nervous."

"I'm not nervous. You're nervous."

"Okay. Yeah. I'm nervous."

He put his hand on her shoulder and squinted at her. "It's all going to go great. You picked a good team. You didn't have the second beer, and you came and got the captain from the storm and his madness."

"Yeah, what's the madness about?" she asked, pulling the beer out of her pocket and popping the lid. She took a swig, and then grinned at the sea.

He shrugged and shook his head, looking down woefully. "I've never won at blackjack. It haunts you after a while."

"Unlucky in cards, lucky in love." She watched a baby sea lion wiggle in the shifting sand at water's edge.

"You get that beer out of Lex's secret, locked cooler?"

"He says it's champagne for the end of the trip. I saw the receipt. It's the nice stuff... I wish I'd gotten this out of it. He won't let anyone touch it." She looked up at him. "You should tell him sharks like it."

"Then he'll dump it all in." Dr. Hammerstein smiled.

"Hey, we just need a way in the locked cooler. I'll take it from there."

He chuckled. "All right, let's go."

"Mind if I power nap for fifteen when we get back?" She tilted her head over at him.

"I allotted you five power naps a day and that's it."

"I'll both tell Lex the sharks like champagne *and* steal the contents when he opens it if you give me six."

"Done."

*

"One time, about 40 years ago," Lex said, stoking the fire in the deck's fire pit, "Great White Death was said to have disrupted a small music festival the locals put on here." He turned, walked back to his deck chair.

Much to his annoyance, before he even got to sit down and really tell this one, Oliver interrupted. "Back to scaring people. Maybe if we were 12."

Joseph laughed. "Let him tell the story."

Lex looked around at all their faces, eyes lingering a little longer on Oliver's pitch-black ones. Did Oliver see what Lex could do to him? No, he couldn't, but some part of him was afraid of Lex. Lex knew it.

Everybody had some sense to stay away at least a little bit unless Lex was careful. Lex knew how to be careful.

He told the story in creatively graphic detail, watching the reactions of the others. Bunny, nothing, as usual. Lost in her booze haze. Aaron was rapt with attention. Dr. Hammerstein ate his hot dog and listened with interest. He knew most of these stories, or had and forgot them. He had known most everything to Lex and had seemed to enjoy telling him shark legends he knew of. Lex loved it.

Melody grinned and laughed at Lex's more descriptive gore-gore, while Chas played on his phone. Oliver all but glared at Lex the whole time, just waiting to speak. *Did he ever listen*, Lex wondered?

He couldn't wait until they all went to sleep. He had plans.

He was going to bring Great White Death.

Diane held his knee the whole time he told the story. Her delicate, thin hand, so pale and pure. He wanted to know her perfectly so very badly.

*

Lex stood farther down the island from the yacht, at a point, and had climbed over some rocks and swam through water to get there. It was the dead of night. This was where he planned to summon Great White Death. He had to test to make absolutely sure he could bring the great white shark. Lex knew his lore. He knew the local witchcraft, and a couple years before the trip, made some visits to less scrupulous "psychic readers" to learn just the right things.

What nobody alive knew about Lex was that he was a killer. He had no problem with this: that he was a killer, not that nobody alive knew. He didn't want them to, though. He'd go to jail, and then he wouldn't get to kill anymore.

He'd hit a snag. An ongoing, brutal reality about his killings that he could hardly live with anymore.

This expedition gave him an answer.

Lex meant it when he told Great White Death's earliest legend. He said that no two make the same sound when utterly tortured. It was true. That's when Lex knew them, truly knew them. Lex only felt he completely understood another human being when they'd reached that point, the point where they were making their own sounds of terror, torture, and insanity…but it was always right before they died.

That was the part that got Lex.

With every single person he murdered, he immediately regretted it if he did it this way. He knew them. *Knew them.* Understood them completely. He loved them unconditionally forever in that moment and didn't want them to die, but they always did. Lex lived with great regrets from his strange, unexamined urge to kill, but much examined urge to feel an awesome understanding of another person.

He wanted to know Diane. He would never kill her, though. He loved her more than life itself. Still, it ate at him. He *could* know her, he just needed to set it up.

Great White Death was the solution.

Lex pulled a plastic bag and a butterfly knife out of his jacket pockets. He unwrapped a limp bat body, pocketed the wrapper, flipped the knife open, and held the knife out over the water, bat body to the blade's side.

He stabbed the bat body in the heart, squeezed the thing just right. Lex knew how to keep blood off himself. The bat's blood fell into the sea.

He tossed the bat body in, took several steps back, and waited.

The wind was fierce now, and rain stung like ice pellets. Little, sharp stabs. The water was rough.

Lex waited.

Time passed. Lex didn't get cold. He stayed alert.

He was a shark lookout.

He saw a large, dark fin, but it had to be literally only a second or two before an enormous great white shark plunged from the sea, gaping mouth wide and ready, teeth glistening in the lightning. Lex couldn't even see anything but its mouth.

That second was enough for Lex to jump back and into the water behind the rock he stood on.

The giant shark mouth closed on empty air and the beast landed on the rock with a thud. His garish mouth opened and clamped shut violently over nothing.

Lex treaded water, heart pounding, knees shaking, and waited with all his calculated patience.

The shark stopped his chomping, realizing there was no meal here anymore, and slid back into the sea.

Lex swam to the next rock, hopped up, then to the next rock, and finally got to land.

He bent over his knees, head up and still staring at the darkness where he had made it happen, fear eating him up. Fear wasn't something he felt very often, and he didn't like it.

But it would be worth it. He had found Great White Death, and his trick was in an old story out of a witch woman's mouth.

He'd done it. This was going to happen. He would know Diane, and she wouldn't have to die if Lex did it just right.

The shark was terrifying. That much was for sure. Great White Death should suit Lex's plans well, as long as he didn't mess it up.

Lex hardly ever made those kinds of mistakes.

CHAPTER TWO – DAY 2

Bunny entered the community cabin of the yacht completely soaked. She stripped off her coat immediately. Even her long, blonde hair, which had been under her hood, was drenched. "Everything's still working right." Diane liked Bunny's soft, high voice.

"We all lost cell signal," Joseph told her as Chas came down behind her, just as wet. Melody handed them clean towels.

"This storm might be too bad for the study," said Aaron after he chomped down a handful of almonds.

"Nah, it'll be ok. We needed it to be rough," Diane told him. She wanted to keep everyone's spirits high.

It was around nine in the morning, and Chas and Bunny had been working since the dark dawn. The cabin they all gathered in to stay out of the storm was full of computer and tech gear. The plan was to get video and audio from all angles on the small stretch of beach Diane and Dr. Hammerstein had been on the day before and look for patterns in the sea lions' behaviors. Diane had this particular interest because sea lions were food for big prey, and predators for small. They would react to a long, rough storm according to their position, and Diane had a few hypotheses they were testing for as to what the sea lions would do. Her specialty was this marine biology subject. Aquatic food chain, basically.

Dr. Hammerstein was still in his sleeping cabin, the only person with a cabin to himself. Everyone else bunked up in twos. Diane was grateful that the university gave them this boat. Big, yet advanced technologically, and made just for a study like this.

"Well, D," said Joseph, smiling at Diane, "now let's watch and see." He gestured to the 10 monitors on the back wall of the cabin.

"I think I'm going to be sick again," Melody said, covered her mouth, and then ran for the bathroom. She didn't have sea legs for being on a boat in weather like this, and she wasn't the only one. Aaron, Joseph, and Bunny were struggling.

Lex was as tough and smooth as always. Diane hated that she found his ability to keep stomach bile down on a yacht in a sea storm sexy. Who was she kidding? Everything about the still-mysterious man was sexy.

Lex stood up from the sofa and pulled Diane to the wall of monitors. The rest of them followed suit and they all watched the sea lions on the screens. Diane was proud that they seemed to have gotten every vantage point on camera. Even the two underwater cameras at the water's edge picked up the swirling madness of a shoreline being ravaged by weather.

The sea lions seemed most concerned with their young. Watching them huddling together in groups, covering the youthful sea lions with their adult, thick girths, made her think of how amazing it was that animals had only their bodies for protection against storms like these. The sea lions' whole feeding, mating, and sleep schedules would become desperate and irregular. People could build shelters, but animals never did. They toughed it out without a complaint. They often didn't make it.

"I see something weird," said Melody behind them. She'd come back from hurling in the bathroom without Diane noticing.

"What'd you see?" said Chas.

Melody eased through the group and to the monitor in the top, left corner. It displayed the southwest side of the sea lions' beach, looking out over the shoreline to the other side of the inlet. It picked up a lot of open water on the island's left side.

"Look, here. It's not there now, but keep looking," said Melody, holding her finger over wild waters in the open sea. "Wait for it. Wait. I saw it." She looked back. "Lex? You especially look."

"Why?" Diane said. "What is it you see?"

"Just..." Melody trailed off, staring at the spot her finger hovered over.

They watched churning ocean.

Nothing happened.

"I don't see a thing," said Oliver. "What did you think you saw?"

"You never see a thing," Melody said. "Be quiet and watch. You'll see them."

"Them?" said Lex, getting closer to the monitor by standing next to Melody.

They watched with nothing but the thunder and rain for sound until Diane saw. She saw *them*. Dorsal fins. Three of them bobbing up from the surface in formation.

"Is that...?" Diane said.

Lex folded his arms across his chest. "My friends," he said, "we have some great whites looking for breakfast."

"Holy crap!" said Melody. "I knew it!"

"We have to wake up Dr. Hammerstein," Chas said.

"I'll get him," said Aaron, and left the room in a hurry. Diane figured he hated missing any of the action, but they really needed the expert. They knew great whites came to the waters of this island, but here and now, first day of the storm... It was almost too good to be true. The life cycle, the food chain's natural ways, could possibly be about to play out. Just what they came for.

"Lex," Diane said. "How big do you think they are?"

He rubbed his chin, dark eyes wide with excitement. "They're young. I'd say about six foot each. If that." He smiled at Diane, then focused back on the three fins now so very close to the beach and the hunkered-down sea lions.

"The water, it keeps washing up and over the sea lions," said Joseph. "Those baby sharks have full access to them."

"Yeah," said Chas, "but Lex, are we in danger? I mean, there's three of them." He wrung the hem of his sweater and water gushed out.

Lex continued staring at the screen as though he hadn't heard Chas, but Diane knew he was putting pieces together through observing before giving an answer. He did that a lot, and some people thought he was being rude, but that was only because they didn't know Lex. He thought before speaking. Always.

"Hey, man. Lex," Chas urged, sounding worried.

Two of the fins submerged and a sudden burst of wild wind blew rain at the camera they watched through. Diane couldn't see anything for a few moments.

"They're not dangerous to us," Lex finally said. "They want the sea lions. They've fed on them here before."

"How do you know that?" asked Oliver. "I mean, you can't just know something like that."

Lex turned his head to Oliver. "Sure, I can." He smiled lazily and relaxed his shoulders while Oliver cocked an eyebrow and tilted his head.

"Probably some legend you dug up off the Internet again."

Lex turned back to the monitor. "See? The wind changed direction. It's blowing the sea up onto the shore again. See the way the fins are lined up? One in front, two in back to either side. I'd bet they're related, born at the same time. Still feeding together. Now, see?" He pointed at the fin in front. "It's waiting to get a good ride onto the beach, and the others wait. That one is the leader. The leader for now, before they become solitary adults."

"Now you know they're related?" Oliver said, then chuckled. "You do love your stories."

"Shut up, Oliver," said Chas. "So, this is what we came for, then."

"Yep," said Lex.

"Yeah," murmured Diane.

They all fell quiet and watched the fins bob in the stormy morning sea. The sea lions had no idea. The anticipation was killing Diane. She wasn't at all squeamish about the massacre that the sharks had in mind, but was rather fascinated with it. They, too, needed something to live on through this storm, and those sea lions were just the thing. The water under the surface would be as rough as above. Their usual fare under the sea wouldn't be available, so they'd attempt a beach attack.

Aaron and a groggy Dr. Hammerstein came in the cabin and stood behind Diane, saying nothing. Dr. Hammerstein wiped his glasses on his sleeve, put them on, and then focused on the monitor with the fins. The sharks were closer to shore now, and it had to be any time that they would attack.

Then, out of nowhere in the gray, swirling world of the monitor, a great white shark that had to be three times bigger than the hunters came out of nowhere. Its dorsal fin showed for a split-second, warning of its size. It headed straight for the shark on the left, and its head surfaced…but it was a gaping hole of a thousand huge, sharp yet ragged teeth.

"What the—?" Melody gasped.

What Diane could make out was tough to see because of the interference from the storm, and it all happened so fast. This new, huge shark mouth collapsed on the smaller shark flanking the left, crushing down on and through its middle, and had to have broken the little great white's back. But this demon shark didn't stop at that. Its jaws kept going and going, and to Diane, it was almost as though the big shark were enjoying tasting the little one. The caught shark's head waved back and forth, mouth open and teeth gnashing at open air, while the big great white let its victim's innards spill into the sea.

It was incredibly fast, and it didn't stop there. In a flash, as soon as the victim shark stopped moving, the giant great white took out the shark on the right in the back in the exact same way, and then sunk below the surface, its fin rising high. It raced through the water toward the shark in front, who had no idea what had just happened.

The giant shark resurfaced, but with the last little shark's tail in its teeth. The baby came almost all the way out of the water. The huge great white gnawed its way up the tail, and then the back of the little shark's head bobbed violently in and out of the water, eyes rolled back, mouth opening and closing, face jerking back and forth.

The big shark devoured the little one from back to front. *No,* Diane thought, *not devoured.* The shark tore it apart by killing it painfully, and of all three of its victims, none seemed to have been eaten. Their body parts were all through the rough water, blood washing the sea black, and shredded shark innards floated violently in the waves. The underwater cameras even picked up baby shark bits and bones.

That shark wasn't feeding. It was destroying.

Diane grabbed Lex's arm. "What is that? What's it doing?"

"Yeah, what the hell?" Chas said.

"That's not how sharks act," said Dr. Hammerstein quietly.

As quickly as the massacre started, it ended, and the massive predator was gone, leaving the pieces of his destructive and bloody slaughter washing in the rough sea as the only thing keeping Diane believing she'd seen what she'd seen.

Diane looked at Lex. His eyes were wide with wonder, as though he'd found a secret treasure.

"Lex. Lex, what is it?" she asked him.

They all turned to look at Lex.

"It's him. That's him. That's Great White Death," was all he said, voice steady, a flat tone.

"That's bullshit," Oliver said. "That's some territory crap. Lex, there's no such thing as Great White Death, idiot."

"Hey!" Diane said.

"It's okay," Lex said, looking in her eyes before turning to Oliver. "Remember, Great White Death most enjoys murdering his own kind."

"That's your shit story. What are you trying to do, scare everybody again? You so, so like scaring people, right? You say it enough." Oliver put his hands on his hips and leaned toward Lex. Lex didn't move an inch. "Shut the hell up and do your job here. What was that? Explain that with your real knowledge."

Lex still hadn't blinked as he stared at Oliver. "It's him. I know it."

"Did you see the size of those teeth?" Aaron interrupted. "I mean...it ripped them to pieces in seconds, and it seemed like a hate killing. He didn't even eat them, not a mouthful. It's freaking creepy, man."

"I know, right?" Melody answered, and then everybody started talking at once. Diane tuned them out and watched Lex. He continued to stare at Oliver in a strange way, his face a mask. Oliver had joined in the cacophony of voices trying to make sense of what they'd just seen, totally forgetting what a dick he'd been to Lex.

Diane could tell Lex hadn't forgotten. She wondered what he was thinking as he watched Oliver with a blank expression.

She was blown away by what they'd all seen, but now her focus shifted. Lex. She saw something different right then. His commenting that the shark murdered its own kind. Murdered, not killed. It ran through her head a few times.

Then she suddenly had that tired feeling, the one she explained as needing power naps for, and forgot about Lex's comment. Time to snap to. She pulled the hair on her forearm hard, eyes watering, and listened closely. *Pay attention*, she told herself. *Focus*.

"Okay," Dr. Hammerstein said loudly. "Calm down, everyone. We're safe on the yacht. No trouble here. We even have some guns if anything gets...too out of hand."

"Guns?" Bunny asked quietly.

Diane knew about the shotguns. There were three of them, and a harpoon. She didn't like guns, but now she felt relief knowing they were there. Her observation of Lex's behavior forgotten, she joined in the conversation about the attack, continually watching the carnage of mess in the sea on the monitors. "I can't wait to watch the feed of the sea lions on the beach. They had to have seen it. There will be some reaction."

It continued on this way through the morning, speculation, re-watching the killings, pulling up footage from other cameras…

Diane couldn't make sense of it. *Murder.* She remembered the thought she'd had just before she almost went out in front of everyone. She thought of Lex and his stories of Great White Death. *Murder.*

CHAPTER THREE — DAY 3

Oliver loved the stuff Aaron brought for the trip. It tasted like lemons, and his brain felt like all the tension it always held could be staved off for the time being.

No more events had taken place the day before, and this was day three of their trip. *Well*, Oliver thought, *no events like whatever that was with the giant great white.* Oliver hadn't ever read about anything like that behavior, and he kept trying to figure it out. He took two hits from the joint when it was his turn. He wanted to stop thinking. It was nice to forget stuff sometimes. "Thanks."

Diane, Lex, Aaron, Chas, Melody, Joseph, and Oliver had piled up in Aaron and Chas' cabin to smoke the two joints Aaron presented to them at the end of a long day of recording raw data and reviewing materials. Oliver was grateful. So was everyone else, or so they said. Everyone but Lex. Lex didn't even say thank you once and he would smoke the most of it. At least, he usually did. Oliver couldn't tell what Diane saw in the creep, and Oliver was certain Lex was just that—a creep. A total creep. Oliver could read people, and he enjoyed knocking people like Lex off their high horse. Maybe he shouldn't do it so much, but people like Lex brought it out in him more than anything. Not one of his traits of pride, but he acknowledged the curiosity behind it. *What will they do?*

He passed the J to Melody and she took a long drag, letting the smoke out of her nose after holding her breath. "It tastes even better if you do that. Mmmm, lemons," she said after, smoke still coming out of her nose and mouth.

"This is some of the stuff I grew. Was hoping it'd be ready for our trip and, hey," said Aaron, grinning. Most of them were grinning and nothing was happening to cause it but Aaron's botanicals. They were on the second joint.

"Good, good stuff. Thanks again, Aaron," Oliver said, glancing at Lex to see if he'd say thank you yet. The rest of them took the cue and said the magic words to Aaron after Oliver did.

It was so easy to influence a group, Oliver thought. Not easy to influence Lex. Oliver didn't necessarily want to influence him. He wanted to make Lex's differences stand out.

"I really like your hair that way," said Melody to Diane. "Like, the layers. Don't get me wrong, I liked it long and all, but it *moves*, you know?"

"Thanks," Diane said with a smile.

"I do, too," said Lex.

"It is so weird seeing you without your makeup on, Melody," said Joseph. "You look nice." Melody always wore thick cat-eye blue-black eyeliner to match her blue-black, chin-length hair.

"I look like ass," she said. Oliver knew Melody couldn't take a compliment.

He had to say so. "Why can't you just say thank you, Melody? He said you look good. You say, thank you. It's easy." Oliver glanced at Lex, smirking to himself.

"Psht," hissed Melody. "I know how to say thank you to a compliment, Oliver Green, I just don't happen to agree with that one. In this weather, well, there's no liquid eyeliner that can withstand the chaos." She passed the joint to Diane.

Diane took a gentle puff as though it were a cigarette, inhaling the smoke into her mouth, then into her lungs, and passed to Lex while holding smoke in.

"Blow it out your nose, D. For real," said Melody.

"Diane won't do that," Oliver said. "It's not ladylike."

Lex chuckled and puffed, letting the smoke out of his nose. "Nice. You're right." He handed the joint to Aaron.

"Yeah, because I'm so ladylike. I'm royalty." She said it while still holding her breath and she sounded like someone saying a prayer on her deathbed.

"You kind of are ladylike," said Joseph. Oliver noticed Lex eye Joseph, and he grinned to himself.

Everyone but Diane fully acknowledged that Joseph was over-the-moon in love with Diane, and Oliver enjoyed watching Lex's reactions to Joseph's fumbling flirting. The creep examined Joseph for a minute while the rest of them told stories of how Diane had been ladylike in the past.

"I know she's a lady, Joseph," said Lex at last. Oliver had been waiting for it. Lex continued. "There's nobody like her, is there?"

Maybe Lex was a little bit like Oliver. Poke the unspoken contention after some thought. He couldn't help but throw his dick out there to say, she's mine, in his usual way. Wait a minute, think, say it so he is being sweet to D but letting Joseph know just how much Lex knows Diane, rubbing it in.

Joseph nodded as he took the J from Aaron. "No way. But really, I've never met two people who are alike. Everyone is so different."

Nice misdirection on Joseph's part, Oliver thought.

They carried on that way until the second joint was less than half-gone, and Chas, who'd been mostly quiet, brought it up. Oliver was sure someone would. Weed? Stuck in a cabin during a sea storm? All of them having witnessed a giant killer great white shark destroy its own kind…?

"Okay, okay. So, for real. Lex. What is *up*? I mean, what do you think's going on with the shark?" Chas inhaled and exhaled quickly, then passed to Joseph, keeping his wide, blue eyes on Lex.

Lex waited dramatically. Oliver wondered why it took the creep so long to get out what he wanted to say sometimes. Diane told Oliver once that Lex gave a lot of thought to what he said so as to be considerate of everyone, but Lex sure as hell wasn't considerate with Oliver. Much the contrary.

"Yeah…so, what? Great White Death again?" Oliver couldn't help himself, nor the sarcasm in his voice.

Lex looked at him. His eyes were red and dry. "Yes."

"Okay, okay," Diane said, waving her hand through the smoky air. "Stop it, you two. We're enjoying a much-needed break. It's keeping some of our stomachs settled from seasickness. Oliver, be quiet and let Lex talk." She frowned at him. He felt a little bad, so he figured he could keep his mouth shut for a bit. He didn't like disappointing Diane. She had always been kind to him, and not many people were.

"Zipped, D," he said, mimicking zipping his lips.

Lex had stared at him the whole time Diane pointed out he was being an ass, expressionless.

"Go ahead, hun," Diane coaxed, rubbing his arm. "What do you think?"

"I think it is the legendary shark Great White Death. I know the shark isn't 400, or that he slaughtered Native Americans on land, a whole society. There are so many stories of this shark."

"Lex loves legends," Diane said, even though they all knew it as well as they knew his name.

"I love legends, yeah, and especially ones about sharks. This one has always fascinated me. The stories are ridiculous, but there are consistencies in all of them," Lex said as Diane handed him the J.

Aaron leaned forward. "Tell us one, man. You finish off that bad boy and tell us a story about Great White Death."

That was the last thing in the whole world Oliver felt like listening to, but he'd zipped. That didn't mean he couldn't let everyone know his misery with his expressions. He scowled at Lex.

Melody chimed in. "Tell us one that makes you think it's him. The shark we saw yesterday."

Lex leaned back and put the paper to his lips, inhaling slowly, seemingly lost in thought.

"Oh," said Diane, sounding pretty blazed, "he's running through them all. It's going to be a good one."

Oliver wanted to unzip so bad, but instead, looked at rosy-cheeked Diane admiring her boyfriend in anticipation, and remembered to use his eyes to show his disdain.

Right then, Lex looked straight at Oliver. "There's one Oliver would like, I think. You know, some say there's something to these sea monster stories, and the military constantly monitors the raging wars of the oceans. Hey, maybe giant killer sharks, conspiracy of the essence of reality, and secret military involvement for another night."

They all looked at Oliver. He kept his sardonic expression.

"Not going to say anything?" Joseph said with a laugh.

Oliver did the zip motion again and pointed at Diane.

"Okay." Lex put one hand on his stomach, body completely sunken into the bed pillows and blankets of the bottom bunk, the other hand daintily swirling the roach. "In the late 1960s, there was a hippie commune on the shores of the mainland across from Aña Nuevo Island."

Oliver allowed himself an eyeroll, but only because Lex's gaze was aimed at the smoke above his head, and Diane was enraptured with watching Lex just exist.

"Yeah? I like it," said Melody.

"Is there any other place?" Lex asked her, grinning at the smoke. "Anywhere other than here?"

"Absolutely not, man." Aaron began packing a bowl, shaking his head and chuckling.

"The people who lived in the hippie commune were your stereotypical hippie mentality types personified. They smoked...grass." He gasped dramatically.

"They did?" Melody pried, batting her eyelashes. Oliver watched how Diane loved everyone getting excited for Lex's stories. Her grin said it all.

"You bet they did," Lex said. "They believed in love, finding pure, good love, and completing Mother Earth's plan for them by doing this, and then sharing the knowledge."

"It was a cult," Diane said, feigning being shocked.

"It was called Earth's Green Children, or the EGC. None of them were over 30, about 55 men and women. Any orientation went, any clothes. Or no clothes. Earth's Green Children had over 300 members when it happened."

"When what happened?" asked Chas, eyes so red and mind so stoned he very quickly got sucked in for real. He wanted to know. Oliver stifled a groan. Now the whole lot of them would be, too. High vibes. Group think.

Lex looked over at Chas. "In the EGC, there was a man. He was 20. He was in love with a girl. She was 16. She didn't love him back."

Lex took a hot drag to keep the roach lit. Watched the smoke.

"They were close. They were best friends. They smoked almost every bowl together, except for the one she smoked after sex with her husband. She did love her husband, and this man, this 20 year old, knew he had found his pure, good love in her. One day, he could no longer deny she had found her pure, good love in her husband.

"He went to the shaman. He told her how he would never complete any plan except to die. She delved. She found his secret and truth through intensive questioning with the composure of compassion. It was a mask she wore.

"You see, the shaman didn't like this man because he would never complete Mother Earth's plan. She had to get rid of him. He would poison the community." The roach went out, but Aaron passed Lex the glass pipe he'd filled. Lex nodded at Aaron and hit the pipe.

Oliver saw the nod and started paying attention. The hairs on the back of his neck tingled. He felt as tense as a piano string. Lex never thanked anyone for the bowl. Ever. Had he picked up on Oliver's hints about his personal thoughts on that fact?

The hair on his arms rose. He listened, face still and motionless.

Lex exhaled and handed the pipe the Diane, who hit it fast and passed it to Melody, never taking her eyes off her pure, good love, Lex.

"The shaman," Lex continued, "told the man that a revelation would be given to him as to how to go on, fit in society at the EGC on Aña Nuevo Island in a storm on the next new moon, and to offer bat blood to the sea at midnight. She had a winding list of rituals for him.

"The man, so hopeless before, was completely convinced by the shaman, and the man's love and conflict were no match for the shaman's need to keep the community clean.

"He waited, chanting words she told him to recite each night, until the first stormy new moon, and paddled out here that day by himself, as instructed. He was to tell no one of any of it, and he didn't. Telling, the shaman impressed on him, would keep the truth shrouded in mystery until he did, indeed, die. She knew how to word things to scare him, as she did most."

Melody bumped Oliver's shoulder. He glanced at her. Oh, the bowl. He mindlessly took it, puffed, and handed it to Chas. Other than looking over at Melody, Oliver sat straight and watched Lex.

Lex continued, eyes looking at all of them at once, meeting eyes with each of them, hands dancing. "He stood on the southernmost rock and spilled the bat blood, and, as you've heard happening before, Great White Death launched on him. He didn't see or hear it coming. He'd had his eyes closed, as the shaman had told him to do. But he felt it. He then knew he was to get the second of his two options he told the shaman woman about: his death. The pain was so intense and pointedly stabbing that he lost coherent thought immediately. He didn't have the time to feel bad that a shaman had cleansed him from her community. Great White Death chewed the top half of his body for a full minute."

Lex's fingers turned into shark jaws, clamping the smoky air in front of him. "And he screamed. He cried for the shaman woman to save him at his last, some strange part of him somehow still being in there, and then he knew no words. Great White Death mauled him to mince, yet he stayed alive on and on as though the shark were sentient as to what tender part of the human body actually killed a man when shattered last.

"It did end, eventually, and Great White Death slid back into the sea." Lex fell back into the pillows, grinning. "I like that one. I'm sure Oliver liked that one."

Diane groaned. "What's up with the ages? You tell the ages in every one."

"I don't know. That's the way the stories go." He looked at her, still grinning.

"Like, just for that shark, or..." Chas asked, hands out, confused.

"Yeah," Lex told him. "Just for that shark."

"And they're weird ages," said Joseph. "Right?"

"Yeah," Lex said, taking the pipe from Aaron, but passing it to Diane without a puff. "All of them are."

There were the usual things Oliver would say here...for example, "And you memorized the exact ages in all of these stories?" But no. He was at alert. He'd picked up on something, but he couldn't figure out what, and he didn't like it. His sixth sense for what made people tick noticed a simple thing: Lex nodding to Aaron for the bong coincided with his annoyance about how Lex never thanked anyone for smoke.

As usual with Oliver, he'd made a private game out of it, watching people.

He knew then that Lex did that, too, and he was doing it to Oliver, but that didn't explain the goosebumps. The adrenaline.

Whatever it was, Oliver was completely uneasy and needed to be alone.

Oliver waited about five minutes, then played the tired card and escaped without a fuss. Nobody noticed his change in attitude. He didn't know if it was because they couldn't tell or didn't care. That didn't matter. He wanted to get to his cabin and go the hell to bed, figure this out in the dark. He wouldn't sleep until he did.

CHAPTER FOUR

Lex knew Oliver liked that story, but too much. Yeah, and Lex gave too much away. The opportunities were irresistible, but it didn't occur to Lex that Oliver would catch on to his game.

He gave credit where credit was due. Now, how to get Oliver to the water?

He had to think…think fast. Oliver wanted to prove himself all the time, and now he had something to prove about Lex. He would put things together in time. Oliver caught patterns. So did Lex. Lex was sure Oliver was holed up in his bunk trying to figure out why Lex had been toying with him.

Lex was a predator, like a shark. Oliver somehow got it, but didn't quite get exactly what. Not yet. The guy knew Lex was different, but not how different.

Lex was more excited now than he had been before. It was going to happen, happen in a good way. Get to know Oliver? That guy? The emotional potential to feel a complete knowing of Oliver made his thoughts sharp. It would bend his mind, his core being. Lex started sweating lightly in hopeful anticipation.

Lex needed to make it so that Oliver first had something to prove to Lex before he had something to prove *about* Lex, and that something needed to be proven on Aña Nuevo Island's beach, away from the yacht.

Oliver's weakness for Lex to exploit was his curiosity. That's where he would start. He had to fix this fast.

He picked up the pace as he walked to his cabin. He had purpose, and time could move out of the way.

He was going to get to test his plan, see if it would work the way he thought. He would test it on Oliver.

He was going to feel *it* soon. Lex wiped his hairline of sweat.

He had left the smoky cabin ten minutes after Oliver. He'd told Diane he was tired. He'd kissed her goodbye. She'd smelled lovely.

He entered his and Diane's cabin and went to his cooler, unlocked it, and pulled out a bagged, fresh bat body. Locked the cooler up tight after and pocketed the key.

He then went to Diane's suitcase. He knew where she always kept a personal stash and a pipe for after her power naps when she woke up irritable. She had special stuff, something Oliver wouldn't be able to resist. Everyone knew Diane's special stuff.

He packed the pipe, stood up, and then scooped up her whole jar of bud. Lex was about to make a peace offering. It had to be bountiful to be tempting enough.

*

"Well, that was weird," said Melody after Lex left.

"What, Oliver shutting up or Lex leaving before it's all smoked?" Diane said. She'd enjoyed herself tonight.

Melody looked at Diane on the bottom bunk where she'd been snuggled up with Lex, then at the others. "You didn't catch that?"

"What?" Aaron said, cocking his head. He looked 15 when he was high. *Maybe,* Diane thought, *it was the baby face mixed with the way his eyes unfocused a little.*

Melody shook her head. "It's like, weird. I don't know. Could be it's just me. Lemon flavor. Go figure."

"Yeah," Aaron said with complete seriousness. "Lemon flowers make you make no sense."

Chas cracked up.

They goofed off some more for a while, all knowing they needed to get sleep, but enjoying not having seasickness for a while.

For Diane, it had been hard to stay asleep after seeing those young great whites massacred by the giant one. She kept waking up from dreams where she was the young shark in the lead of the three, and the giant great white was chewing up her tail...and then she'd jump awake, stiff. It even happened during the many power naps she took. All her sleep had ended that way since.

It wasn't the gore. It wasn't the shock sensation. That giant great white shark was out there. It was something none of them had said aloud. Diane knew they all wanted to be scientists and not get carried away by thinking a great white shark could take down this vessel and eat them all because it was insanely bloodthirsty and evil. Weren't they all questioning it, though? At least a little?

Diane was.

Soon, Aaron and Chas were talking about politics, and Joseph moved to sit next to Melody on the floor. He didn't like political "discussions," either. And he'd do the quotes, if he said it aloud.

Diane listened to Melody talk about some grants she found that they might be able to use for the next trip. Often, when Melody and Diane stayed up late together at their apartment from month one, they'd scheme up research projects to get grants for so they could travel and get real, hands-on experience. What they were doing here on Aña Nuevo Island was their first dream-come-true, their scheme coming to fruition.

Diane was having a hard time concentrating, and she wanted to pay attention. This stuff was her passion. Melody always had good ideas, just like the trip they were on now.

Focus, she thought, and said the first thing that came to her foggy mind. "That was a great idea."

Melody paused, eyes pointed up, trying to remember a figure for one of the grants. Diane had had to say something, anything, engage in conversation. Focus. Stay awake.

She watched Melody, who whipped her head around. "What?"

"Your idea for this trip. It was a great idea." Diane smiled up at her, letting her head roll to the side on her pillow so she was facing Melody. "One of those nights. You were doing this and that's how we got this one on Aña Nuevo Island. Hey...hey!" Diane slapped the bed, grinning. She had her focus back in a flash.

"What?" Melody said, eyes wide.

"We did it. We did it." Diane laughed.

"Oh. Oh, yeah. It's actually happening. I mean, we talked about it actually *going* to happen, but right now it's *happening*, happening." She held out her hand. "High five."

Diane tried to match Melody, but slapped her forearm instead of her palm.

"Try again tomorrow?" Diane asked, flopping her hand around.

"Yeah. We'll nail it. But we have to give Lex some credit. If it weren't for him, I wouldn't have had the idea, when you really think about it." She shrugged.

"What do you mean?" Joseph joined in. Diane wondered why he'd been so quiet. Maybe Melody intimidated him in her raw form. The two had never spent much time together. Although Melody was outgoing, she was hard to get to know well. She kept everyone at a distance.

Melody turned to him. "Well, Lex gave me a pamphlet on research done on Aña Nuevo Island with about four others he picked up while backpacking in California two summers ago, saying maybe Diane and I could work an angle on the requisites."

"That's right," Diane said. "I remember that. Long, long before Lex and I became hot and heavy, Joseph," she told him, "Lex would sometimes come over with Aaron and catch us talking about the scheme."

"The scheme to travel under the guise of intensive, extensive, time-consuming research?" He smiled, raised his eyebrows.

"Exactly," Diane said.

"Yeah, and Lex gave me a handful of grant pamphlets and a few of local places that allow research, that are only for research like Aña Nuevo," Melody explained.

Joseph nodded.

Diane sat up, rubbed her eyes. "Did you say he gave you a pamphlet on Aña Nuevo Island specifically?"

Melody turned back to Diane. "Yeah. I still have it. It stood out to me. I think it's because he told me one of those Great White Death legends. It was another 14-year-old girl in 1865 marrying a 24-year-old woman or some crap like that." She shook her head. "I totally forgot that. I'm so used to Lex trying to scare me with his stories about shark legends that they all run together, kind of like remembering a book."

"He loves to tell his lore," Diane said quietly. "He travels to different places that have sharks, goes to the dock bars, and asks locals for shark stories."

"You're kidding," Joseph said.

"Nope," Diane said.

Melody put her hand on his shoulder. "Mysteries abound, young Joseph."

He laughed. Diane liked his laugh. He sounded like he self-consciously felt like he sounded stupid when he laughed, which made him sound really dumb. That made her laugh every time he did. Infectious.

"Great White Death," he said. "What a crazy story, but to see that shark out there. I mean, I don't know what to think about that."

"To be honest," Melody said in a low voice. "I don't get scared by much. I like horror movies and books. Fun! That huge great white scared me a little." She looked back and forth at them. "Either of you get scared?"

Joseph shrugged. "Well, maybe there was an element of surprise."

"Really?" Melody sounded like she didn't believe him.

Diane answered for him. "Melody, was it the guts? The blood that scared you?"

She took a sip of her bottled water. "You know, I think it might be. In movies and books, it's not real and I'm never tricked into thinking it is. This was real." She looked at Diane. "You and Joseph get into the gutsy wutsies all the time, so maybe not for you?"

Joseph said, "Yeah, that's it for me. Plus, seeing it on a screen makes it seem not real."

Diane looked at the bottom of the bunk above her, then softly said, "I wasn't scared then, but it's spooked me after."

She was team leader. She had to be the toughest one. Still, this was her roommate and her lab partner of several years. She bit her lip, wondering if she should mention the dreams, her worries and irrational fears, and screw the stable boss act.

Melody didn't give her time to say any of it if she'd wanted to, and relief from avoiding the decision flowed through Diane. "I'm glad I'm not the only one. That was some stuff to see for yourself," Melody said, shaking her head and closing her eyes. "I did not like it at all. I don't know how you two spend so much time studying biology-biology. Bodies and body parts. They're disgusting."

So it went until way, way too late, and Diane felt her vision fade… This time, she couldn't focus. She couldn't stop it.

When she went out like this, she was gone. She could hear everything around her, but she was asleep. It hardly ever went this way. She usually could focus, focus, and nobody would know.

Somewhere in their conversation, she'd fallen out hard, and nobody could wake her up. She felt them shaking her, calling her name, laughing that she smoked too much.

Joseph volunteered to carry her back to her cabin, and Melody guided the way.

Inside her cabin, Diane felt Joseph tuck her under the covers of the bottom bunk. "Where's Lex?" Joseph asked Melody.

"Beats me."

Diane wanted to reach out to where Lex slept, but her body wouldn't allow it. Paralyzed, and her ability to hear and feel fading, she drifted.

She hadn't told a soul on the trip about her narcolepsy. Not a person in her college life had a clue.

She never would have been given the funding if the school knew. She might not have gotten her first scholarships in field research. Nobody could know.

Her power naps were considered a quaint curiosity or quirk, and Diane's sleep issues couldn't always be hidden. She'd done well this far with quaint and quirky because she was good at what she did scholastically, and had been working with sleep disturbances her whole life without having to explain them to too many people. She had tricks, like pulling arm hair or engaging someone in conversation, until times when she had to explain away an unavoidable doze by her quirky need for a power nap.

She let her concerns slide away. She would sleep well, and she felt safe with Joseph's hand on her arm, hearing him say goodnight. It was as if he knew she still heard him.

She might not have the dream.

Once she heard the cabin door close, she let herself go full-force dead body sleep, with her last sentient thought being, *please don't have the dream.*

*

Lex knocked gently on Oliver's cabin door. Waited. Knocked again.

"Sleeping, go away," Oliver called from within the room finally.

"It's Lex."

A pause, and then, "Seriously, man, I'm tired."

"Oliver," Lex said, loudly enough so Oliver could hear, but as quietly as possible so as not to draw attention from anyone who happened to be nearby. "I came to say I'm sorry."

He waited, listening. Nothing.

"I have a peace offering. Please," Lex said, leaning into the door to see if he could hear Oliver moving.

After a moment, Oliver called out, "What kind of peace offering?" He sounded suspicious. Lex needed him not to be suspicious.

"The kind Diane keeps for her naps." He waited. Nobody could resist Diane's special stash. Especially not Oliver. He didn't talk about his love for smoke, but the only times Lex saw Oliver relax and his overworked brain slow down was when he smoked.

He heard movement from the other side of the door and took a step back. A couple of minutes later, Oliver opened the door a crack and peeked out at him. "Why?" was the first thing he said.

Lex widened his eyes, straightened his back. "Because I'm an ass. I've always been an ass to you." He held up Diane's jar.

"You're just now realizing it?"

"Diane. She points it out, asks me not to antagonize you." Lex looked down submissively. "She's right. I do it, and it's not right. I'm sorry."

Oliver opened the door. "Okay, Okay. I accept your peace offering. Come on in and let's talk before Joseph comes back. Don't want to use up all of D's goods."

Lex looked up and smiled meekly. "Thanks, man." He went inside and Oliver closed the door behind him. He sat on the bottom bunk and pulled out the packed pipe, letting the jar slide out of his pocket so Oliver would see how much he had. Now, it was time to play. Lex loved this part of it. The game. He had a task—get Oliver so stoned he made poor decisions, get him so convinced Lex was the best friend he never had that he would go out to Aña Nuevo's beach in a raging storm in the middle of the night to bond with his newfound bestie.

They finished the bowl and packed two more. Lex had adrenaline on his side, so he didn't get too buzzed. He took smaller hits once he saw Oliver getting more blitzed, and they talked. Well, Oliver talked as Lex asked questions. Lex knew that was how people felt like they were bonding. He asked them questions about everything and listened, and then they felt understood, appreciated. With Oliver, Lex thought it might be hard with their history and his new seed of suspicion from earlier in the night, thus Diane's sleep stuff to loosen the grip of Oliver's dead-on paranoia.

It had to be two in the morning when Lex thought he had an in. Oliver's eyes were bright red and he smiled as he recounted a fishing trip with his now-dead father where he caught the big one. Those fishing trips, he confided in Lex, were what got him into marine biology. Oliver even smiled when describing his father, and his dry eyes watered a little as he talked about the man passing away from aggressive lung cancer when Oliver was 15. Oliver had been in the hospital room the moment he died. He told Lex he'd never felt anything like it, how he'd known his father was no longer in that body in that instant.

Lex had him.

Lex was acting completely stoned like Oliver, but he wasn't in the least. It had taken time, but the challenge was delicious. Lex knew it. He had him. Now was his in. "Oliver, you're such a cool guy. I mean it. I wish I'd gotten to know you better sooner, and I hate that it took my girlfriend getting mad at me for being a dick to realize I needed to fix it. That I didn't give you a chance, a basic courtesy. But you know what?"

"What?" He wiped his eyelashes of moisture left from talking about his father's death.

"I'm glad it happened. I'm glad I came tonight. Thank you for accepting my peace offering. I know I don't deserve the chance."

Oliver waved a hand through the air. "Old news. All gone, man. I never could understand you, tried to figure you out...but..." He trailed off, staring into space.

"Tell you what," Lex said, acting excited. "Let's do something for your dad. For your dad's memory."

Oliver looked over at him. "What? Like what?"

Lex smiled. "Like, a fishing trip. Like, an aquatic adventure."

Oliver laughed. "Aren't we on one right now?"

"I mean, you and me. Right now. Let's go out on the island and laugh at the gods in the storm."

Oliver spewed out a stream of smoke as he laughed. "You're crazy."

Lex sat up, eyes wide, palms sweating. "It would be great. No city lights, pure darkness. A wild sea storm. It'll be like we're natives. From way back. It'll be like a ceremony, a ritual. In your dad's memory. From what you've told me, he'd like that."

Oliver blinked, his newfound comfort in Lex's presence disrupted as he eyed Lex. Lex saw that same suspicion Oliver had in the other cabin when Lex had nodded thanks to Aaron. He'd done it because it was so very obvious to him that Oliver was annoyed by Lex not doing something like that. Oliver's expressions, his comments, so easy to read... And now, Lex worried he had jumped the gun. "It'll be fun. I promise." He held his breath.

Oliver bent over his knees and shook his head. "I don't know. It's a bad storm. But… you're right. Dad would like that. He would like me doing something like that in any circumstance. He used to say I didn't take enough chances and risks."

"You made him sound like an adventurer. That's why I thought of it." Lex smiled at him as Oliver sat straight and looked at him, thinking. Lex waited, making himself breathe normally. He almost had the guy. And that meant he was one step closer to the knowing. Nothing Oliver had told him as they "bonded" over Diane's smoke was surprising to Lex, but if Great White Death got ahold of Oliver, Lex's whole world of who Oliver was would open up like a blooming flower.

"You're right." Oliver shot up out of the bed in a flash. "Yeah. Yeah, why not? Adventure. Sea storm so bad there's no cell phone signal out here. You know what, Lex? It's on." He turned to Lex and grinned, all suspicions forgotten. "Let's do it. Let's go."

"Excellent."

*

Lex brought Oliver to the farthest point of Aña Nuevo Island from the yacht. He had made Oliver think they needed to sneak, that everyone would think they were crazy if they caught Lex and Oliver doing this. Besides, Lex had pointed out, it was their thing. Their moment. Private. Oliver had bought the new friendship olive branch with a $100 bill, and they sneaked off the yacht in the storm without anyone seeing them.

Now, with the wind whipping their drenched coats, hoods off and both of their hair flying around in the wind like seaweed under the sea before them, Oliver held up the beer he'd snagged for the adventure and cried out, "Yes! This is just what I needed!"

Lex grinned. "Me too." Behind his back, he slid the bat body out of its bag and sliced its chest open. He worked his way around to facing Oliver, hands still behind his back, and said, "Make a wish, say a prayer. Everything changes tonight." He tossed the bat body into the sea behind him and grabbed Oliver's shoulders. "Go. Go out to the water's edge on this rock and curse those gods. Become a god!" he called out to be heard over the thunder.

Oliver's eyes were wide with chemical influence and heartfelt joy as a flash of lightning lit his face for a moment. "Yes. Yes! Absolutely!" Lex dropped his arms as Oliver went around him and stood as close to the rough water as he could. He held his hands out from his sides, palms up, dropping his beer bottle, and turned his face to the sky to rain down upon him.

Lex knew it would be any minute. He had to be completely alert, because Great White Death wouldn't stop at Oliver's tasty flesh. That shark would go after Lex in an instant at seeing him. Lex *knew* that beast would somehow intuit that there were two feasts to be had when he was summoned and surfaced. Great White Death saw all.

Lex stepped back, watching Oliver cry in the rain. *Probably releasing all his pain from his father's death memory*, Lex thought, watching the water's surface closely for the fin before the attack.

The anticipation killed Lex. His life's purpose of knowing another person completely was about to be realized again. This was what drove him. He was about to have that knowing. He was going to feel true actualized purpose, but he had to keep his wits so that Great White Death didn't get him, too.

And then, Lex saw the tip of a large fin pop out of the sea just before Oliver, who had his eyes closed. Lex scooted back a ways onto the island, staring over his shoulder. He had to stay in hearing distance which, in the storm, meant staying a little too close for comfort. It was worth the risk.

Oliver must have looked just as the enormous great white shark slammed out of the sea, aiming for his prey with a wide-open mouth full of gleaming, sharp, and deadly huge teeth. His head bobbed with disbelief.

He screamed, "Lex! Fuck!"

It was too late. As the curse left his lips, the great white shark of legend gnashed its ragged, huge bite onto Oliver's legs and twisted its head, jerking Oliver off the ground. Oliver wailed in shock and pain.

Great White Death flipped him onto his stomach, and began systematically destroying Oliver's legs, crunching them to mush. Lex saw blood squirting out from the new holes in Oliver's lower extremities. Then he heard... He heard Oliver's true voice, his shrieks of terror and unbearable fear, pain.

Lex stared, mouth open, waiting for it as he listened.

The world is against him... Time is motionless, yet malleable... He knows what the wolves feel when they howl at a half moon...

Great White Death wasn't satisfied with his prey's anguish. It wasn't enough. The shark let go of Oliver's legs, slipped back into the sea for a breath of water, and in a flash, lunged out of the sea, aiming for Oliver's arm and side.

One of Oliver's legs was completely chewed off and lay discarded and unneeded by the great white. The other bent a million ways. There was so much blood, dark, dark blood Lex saw in the light of the constant lightning.

"No, no… No!" Oliver wailed as the shark clamped onto his arm and ribs, crunching him just so that he suffered enormously, but didn't yet die.

It all happened so fast, but Lex rode the high. He was hearing it. He was knowing Oliver as the young man begged incoherently for it to stop. His good arm flopped uselessly against the shark's pointed nose in an instinctual effort to stop it, stop it all.

He knows nothing… He knows too much… He sees mirrors and doesn't recognize the face within… Books and knowledge are the world… Everything can be discovered…

This was it. Lex's eyes rolled back in his head as he soaked in Oliver, the real Oliver. First, the pain and isolation, then, like all of them at the end, the hope. The joy. The unique love within.

The rain spread Oliver's blood all over the rock as Lex looked again. Oliver's face was turned toward him, eyes wide, tongue hanging out. He knew nothing of reality now, just absolute pain, just absolutely the end.

The shark chewed on Oliver's side, and Lex heard the crushing of his ribs, one by one. Blood pumped out of him in all directions.

Oliver let out his last squeals before his lungs collapsed. He writhed in the beast's grueling death grip, his last movements automatic, his mind gone to the pain and the end, so near.

He is the only one… He walks the path of gods… They teach him the ways of patience… The ways of virtue… He follows with joy, relief… They are always with him… They always have been… He knows ecstasy…

He then knew death as Great White Death impaled his head with one last, hard bite to Oliver's skull. His brains popped out, spraying into the night like the devil's fireworks.

Lex was electric, covered in rainwater and sweat. He, too, knew ecstasy, and he loved Oliver so very much. No, he was one with Oliver, and walked with the gods with him.

Lex fell to his knees, overwhelmed by the knowledge of Oliver's very core being, and felt deep compassion and companionship with the man he once found to be horribly annoying.

He covered his face with his hands and wept.

The ground before him trembled. Lex's head snapped up.

The huge great white had slid across the rock, and his snapping, vicious mouth was a few feet away from Lex.

He fell backward, and scrambled on his hands and butt away, away, terror gripping him.

Great White Death followed, his tail fin the only part of him in the water now.

"No!" Lex cried out, horrified. Going from pure, unaltered joy of fulfilling his life's greatest pleasure to near-insane fear made him stop and vomit all over the front of his jacket and pants.

The shark was a foot away, and that awful mouth kept trying to inch closer, never stopping its dreadful snapping. Lex could hear the spiky teeth each time the shark bit down, and it sounded like the ocean itself's own storm, its own thunder. Great White Death was its lightning.

Lex flipped over and jumped up, running for his life without looking back, feeling like the shark was right on his heels with those awful teeth gnashing for him, hearing them crash like a night terror's scream.

He ran all the way to the lighthouse keeper's broken home without looking back, panting, yet hardly breathing, his terror was so intense.

He jumped inside a broken window, and rolled across the creaking floorboards inside, and then stopped. Just stopped.

The shark couldn't get him in here. He'd made it.

He was safe.

Lex got up, caught his breath, and inched to the broken window, looking out.

There was no sign of the great white, and no sign of Oliver. Great White Death must have dragged Oliver's body into the depths with him when he went back to his sea, and Lex was grateful.

The rain would wash away Oliver's blood and leftover innards. All Lex had to do was get back to the yacht and into bed with Diane without being seen.

He went out the back door of the house, and slowly walked to the other side of the island in the downpour. He felt the sadness, the regret. Oliver was a wonderful man, a great person. If only Lex had known him like that when he was alive, but no. Nobody knew those things about Oliver but Lex, and nobody ever would.

It wasn't something that could be told, either, not that Lex could tell anyone. But the depression was setting in, and Lex wished Oliver could have somehow made it. They could have been friends for real, good friends. The best. Oliver was pure and good. Lex admired him so very much.

As he climbed the ladder to the yacht's deck quietly, he felt a chill up his spine as he remembered seeing Oliver's brains squirt out as the shark finished him.

Lex underestimated the beast's blood lust.

Great White Death had almost had him.

That couldn't happen again.

Lex knew now, though, that his plan to know Diane yet save her in time to survive was possible. The killer great white delivered to Lex what he himself had only been able to get out of his victims with his own hands and tools.

Yes, his truest dream would come true, but he had to be doubly careful. If that meant killing everyone but Diane, then so be it. He wasn't going to let this golden opportunity pass, and the only way it would was if the shark outmaneuvered him and got him, too.

CHAPTER FIVE – DAY 4

"Has anyone seen Oliver?" Joseph asked as he entered the working cabin of the yacht the morning of the fourth day of the expedition.

Diane sat up from being slumped at her desk. Joseph sounded upset. "No, why? Is everything okay?" First, Lex had been moody and depressed for no reason when she was waking up, and now Joseph, always so balanced and even, was in distress. This trip wasn't what Diane expected. It was supposed to be the scheme. Fun. Enlightening.

Chas also turned from a computer. "What's up, man?"

Joseph sat on the couch, leaning forward and rubbing his hands together, eyeing them each one at a time before talking. "Oliver wasn't in our cabin when I got in last night. He wasn't there when I woke up, either." He looked down. "I just have this bad feeling."

Diane instantly thought of the shark. The giant great white. She didn't know why. It was a ridiculous, irrational fear. There was no way Oliver had gone out to the water and gotten eaten by the monster. "He didn't leave a note or anything?"

"No," Joseph said, still gazing down. "I looked around the boat. I can't find him. The others aren't awake. I mean, he could have bunked up with someone else. Maybe he woke up Dr. Hammerstein and had one of those long, philosophical discussions with him. You know how he does that. I didn't check Melody's or Dr. Hammerstein's cabin, and you're here, Chas, and you haven't seen him. He wasn't in your cabin." He looked up hopefully. "Or could he have been and you didn't know?"

Who is he kidding? Diane thought. Those sleeping cabins were tiny. Joseph was grasping at straws. "Well, let's go wake them up. We have to see if he's in one of their rooms if you haven't found him anywhere else."

"Yeah," Chas said. "Sorry, man. He isn't in our cabin unless he's under Aaron's bunk." The joke fell flat, and they all stood up to go wake the others.

The storm rocked the yacht like it was a flurry in a shaken snow globe. After waking everyone, and all of them scouring the yacht for Oliver, Diane's worry deepened. They couldn't find him anywhere onboard.

"We have to check the island," said Dr. Hammerstein after they'd reconvened in the main working cabin. The monitors with the sea lions were forgotten. Their project abandoned.

Melody looked out a porthole at the island and rain instead of said monitors in response to Dr. Hammerstein's comment. "Who's going to do that?"

The professor cocked his head at her. "All of us."

Melody turned away from the porthole. "I'm not going out there," she said quietly.

Diane examined her. She was spooked, Diane realized. "What is it, Melody?"

Her friend clenched her hands, shook them nervously. "That—that thing is out there."

"Thing?" said Aaron. "You mean, the great white? The shark?"

Of course, Diane thought. Melody had already expressed how the shark had scared her. Flashes of Diane's nightmares of being a baby shark chewed up alive from back to front by the killer sea creature passed through her mind. She hadn't had the dream when she woke that morning.

She turned to Lex. He still looked depressed. "Lex," she asked him, "will you go look? Maybe you and Joseph? Someone?"

"Of course. Yeah," Lex told her, and then smiled weakly. She wished she understood him better. Why was his mood so low? He'd stayed in bed awake, reading a book about shark feeding habits in the South Pacific, as Diane dressed that morning and went about work. When she'd asked him if he was coming with her, he'd told her he had a massive headache, and it would be a while before he could focus.

A thought occurred to her. How could he have been reading with the supposed raging headache?

The question seemed pointless as Joseph distracted her with, "I'll go, of course. Lex and I will find him if he's out there."

"Alright, then," Lex said, nodding at Joseph. "Let's suit up. Time's wasting."

"Oh my God," Bunny hissed. It took them all by surprise. Bunny had said few words the four days they'd been there, and she sounded horrified. "Look, look!"

Diane turned. Bunny stood in front of the monitors, hand held out, pointing at the monitor showing the edge of the beach where the sea lions weathered the storm. But it wasn't anything the sea lions were doing that had her attention.

It was a giant shark fin torpedoing toward the island, and in an instant, the huge great white shark slammed onto the beach, slid up the loose rocks, mouth ready and open for breakfast. It scooped up two sea lions in one bite, and even in the thick rain, Diane saw blood squirt out of the sides of its mouth as it chewed them both at the same time. They squealed in terror, so loudly all of them heard it in the yacht even though they were yards away and the storm raged. The shark kept biting and biting, and it seemed like the sea lions would never die. Their beach was soaked in bright red blood, and finally the shark literally spit them out and slipped backward into the sea.

Then, almost right away, the great white launched at the beach again, this time filling its maw with two baby sea lions and their mother. As it opened and closed its horrid mouth on their squawking bodies, Diane saw the two little ones impaled on two different enormous teeth. The mother sea lion was getting it even worse as the shark devastated first her tail, then her middle, spilling her guts across the beach.

"Jesus Christ!" Melody yelled.

The impaled baby sea lions wriggled in death spasms of pain as the shark released the now-dead mother and dropped her to the ground. It then slid back into the water, taking the babies with it, still stuck to its teeth.

The water settled back to a stormy sea as though nothing had happened. The beach was flooded with blood and sea lion parts.

"That's the same one," Joseph said. "That's the big one, the one Melody's so scared of." He stopped, then added, "My God."

Bunny finished his thought. "Lex?" She looked at him. "Lex, are some of those stories true?"

Lex straightened up. "Great White Death?"

A hush fell over the cabin.

"It didn't even feed," Dr. Hammerstein murmured.

Lex said, "It's him. It's Great White Death."

Diane stared at him. Had he lost his mind? He was dead serious, but there was a little spark in his eyes that hadn't been there since the night before. Why was that? What they'd just seen was horrible. It was as if the idea that his legendary shark being here, now brought him out of the funk he'd been in since Diane woke up and he was lying next to her, reading.

That was weird, even for Lex.

"No. No way," said Chas. "That's not right. That's just a shark with rabies or something." Another joke that fell on dead ears. Chas had struck out in trying to lighten the atmosphere yet again.

"Yeah," Aaron said, "it doesn't, I mean. It can't be. That's a sea story. But look at the way it slaughtered them. It's like the shark in the legends. Killing for the thrill of it, Lex said."

"Oliver could be out there. With that," Bunny whispered.

Diane watched Lex as he turned to Joseph. "Well, we better go now. The great white shark had his fun for now. It's the perfect time to look for Oliver." He seemed more concerned saying Oliver's name aloud, which was strange. Some kind of…was it tenderness?…when saying "Oliver." Lex didn't care for the guy, but maybe, considering what they'd all just seen on the monitor, Lex was worried, too. For Oliver.

But what would Oliver have been doing on the island all night long in this worsening sea storm? And through the early morning? None of it made sense.

"Yeah," Joseph answered him. "Let's go." He turned toward the stairwell. Lex followed him.

"Wait," Diane said, a thought occurring to her. "Lex, you weren't there when Joseph got me to bed. Did you see Oliver last night?"

Joseph turned around, looking at her curiously. "You were dead asleep. How'd you know—?"

Diane had forgotten herself and almost let too much of a hint out about her narcolepsy. "I was just…you know. Dozing, out of it, but I remember." She looked at Lex, trying to change the subject back to Oliver. "Did you? Did you see him?"

Lex shook his head. "No."

Melody cocked her head, short hair swinging with the sudden move. "Where were you? I thought you said you were tired, going to bed."

Lex shrugged. "I couldn't sleep so I went on deck, drank a couple beers."

"In this storm?" Melody prodded. Diane heard suspicion in her voice.

"I was on the bridge."

"Oh. And you didn't see Oliver at all?" Melody continued.

"No. No sign of him." He turned back to Joseph. "Come on, time's short. Great White Death will come back once he's bored again."

"Stop calling it that," Melody told him. "It's creepy."

Lex looked over his shoulder at her. "It's really creepy." He sounded strange to Diane, but she couldn't put her finger on what it was. She felt a dizzy spell coming over her at the thought of Lex going out there with that thing in the waters. Those deep ocean waves, where nobody could see underneath. That thing could be anywhere, anytime, and nobody would see it until it was too late.

"Lex," she said. "Don't get close to the water. Please. You all saw how far away those sea lions were. The shark just flew up there. It was like it breathed air. Like it didn't care if it suffocated. Please, both of you. Stay away from the shoreline."

"This whole tiny island is a shoreline," said Chas, making Diane feel dizzier. The urge to sleep was overpowering.

Focus, she told herself, and dug her fingernails into her upper arm. She hadn't realized she had her arms crossed, gripping near her shoulders. The giant shark had gotten to her, its second slaughter even more callous than the first. She agreed with Joseph. It was the same shark, for sure. She knew it.

Focus. *Focus*. Her thoughts grew hazy and she sat down.

"You okay, D?" asked Melody.

"Just…overwhelmed is all. Worried."

Dr. Hammerstein sat next to her. "Take it easy. Why don't you try napping? Power nap? Like you do when you're overworked? Stressed out? Think you could just stretch out? Then they'll be back before you wake up, probably finding Oliver in that lighthouse keeper's place. From what I smelled last night, the bunch of you might have driven him to such an altered state that he thought it would be fun to spend the night there. Could be exactly it."

He could have, but Oliver was a creature of habit. Unlikely, but she supposed it was possible.

Diane so wanted to do that—have a quirky power nap. It would be easy, and here was Dr. Hammerstein practically handing her the opportunity to give into sleep. "I don't know."

Dr. Hammerstein stood up. "Here, stretch out your legs. Put your head on this pillow. Relax, D."

Everything was going black on her. "Okay, okay. Yeah. Stress. Lex," she said, looking up at him as she took the whole couch up, voice slurring as sleep started overcoming her functioning. "Be careful. Bring Oliver back."

"You two, hurry," said Dr. Hammerstein.

Diane closed her eyes and all was nothingness in an instant, yet she stayed conscious in her mind, hearing the people around her worry aloud.

She decided to give in, and let her unusual sleep take her completely.

*

Diane woke to Lex shaking her shoulders. "Diane, hey. Diane."

She slowly opened her eyes. Shit. She had that awful nausea she got sometimes from her naps. "Ungh..."

"You okay?" Lex asked. "Come on, sit up."

She slowly did, holding her stomach. The others were all around her, and they looked upset.

Except for Lex. He was blank. Diane had seen him like that before, and her best guess had always been that Lex did it when he was trying to hide strong emotion.

"Lex? Mel? What's going on?" she asked, rubbing her eyes as her heartrate picked up. She looked from face to face.

"They found something," Melody said softly. Diane watched her. She was scared to death, white as a lily.

"Oliver?"

Lex sat next to her and took her hand. "We didn't..."

Joseph sat on her other side. "We looked everywhere, and then I saw it. I don't know how. I mean, the weather. But at the edge of the sea on the other side of the island, well. Well. I saw something and went to look. I was careful, because it was so close to the water, and..."

Diane was wide awake, stomach churning. "What? What did you find?"

Lex squeezed her hand and looked at the carpet.

Bunny answered. "They found Oliver's leg. Just his severed leg." Her voice was as dead as a dog day.

Diane stared at Lex. "What? His…leg? Is that true?"

Lex looked her deep in the eyes. She felt his love for her, his gentle side he rarely let show. "It'll be okay."

"No. No! That's not right! It couldn't be him. It couldn't be his. It was someone else's leg. It has to be." She refused it outright. Her stomach cramped worse. This was too much.

"Babe, breathe."

She snapped out of it, accepting the reality as fast as she'd dismissed it. "We have to leave. We can't call out for help. Even the boat's radio is out. We have to go, go now, go back to the mainland. We have to get help. We have to get—" She bent over and dry heaved between her legs.

"It's okay," Joseph said on her other side, patting her back. "Shh, calm down. You're having those nap problems. How you get sick sometimes after them. Come on, Lex. Take her to your cabin, get her feeling better."

Diane felt Lex's fingers tighten around her palm. "Yeah. Yeah, Diane, come on. Let's go."

"Wait, didn't you hear me? We have to sail out right now. No sitting on our asses. Let's go," she said between gasps, eyes watering madly.

"That's the thing," Dr. Hammerstein told her. "The weather is too rough to sail. These reefs, well, there's a good chance we'd breach the hull in these currents."

Diane sat up and stared at him. He was the captain. He knew best. She didn't know a thing about piloting a yacht. "For real?"

"Yeah," Melody said from across the room. Diane looked to her. Her face was drawn down, and she looked like a lost little girl. She'd been crying. "We're stuck here until something changes. We're staying on the boat. That's it. That's what we're doing." She walked over to Diane and put her hand on her shoulder. "Go with Lex. Get your stomach settled. Go on. You have to process."

She stared at Melody. "How long have I been out?"

"Four hours," Melody told her in a soft voice. "We didn't have the heart to wake you up. Wake you up and tell you. Tell you about Oliver." Diane could see she was terrified and brokenhearted. "But then it was so long, and Lex, he said it was time. Time to wake you up and tell you."

"The shark got him? Is that what you're saying?"

"That's our best guess," Chas said. "Aaron?"

Aaron's baby face looked old. "He was pretty fried last night. Got all quiet and left like that. We thought he was being, well, Oliver, all stuck in his head and leaving pissed about something none of us knew about, but maybe, just maybe he smoked too much. Maybe he went out there."

"Why would he do that?"

Aaron looked down. "I—I don't know. It's a guess, that's all."

She looked from face to scared face.

"Okay, yeah. I do need to go to the cabin." She stood, steadying herself against the rough rocking of the yacht and holding her gut. She looked down at Lex. "You stay here. I need to be alone. I need to think."

"Diane, please," Lex started, but his heart wasn't in it. To her, it seemed like he said it because he felt like he was supposed to. She could tell he didn't want to go.

Maybe he was afraid, too. Maybe he didn't want to leave the main cabin. Maybe he was a coward and needed to be surrounded by people instead of comforting her.

Well, that was fine. Just fine. Fury blazed through her. "I'm going. Please," she said, turning to Dr. Hammerstein. "Please get us out of here the first break you see. At no time do we all sleep at the same time. Always two people awake. Always…"

"D," Joseph said. "It's okay. You're right. That's what we'll do."

"Okay, okay. I'm going." Irrational anger that Lex wasn't insisting he go with her filled her even though she sincerely didn't want him to come. She didn't look at him again. "I just want to be alone for now, okay? Okay?"

"Yeah." Lex was trying to catch her eye, but she wasn't having it. She stormed out of the cabin and down the hall to her sleeping quarters.

Once inside, she collapsed on the bottom bunk, put her head in her hands, and let her shock turn to instant grief. She sobbed harder than she had in years. Oliver. Dead. His leg left on the beach.

That shark. That god-awful great white shark. It did like killing. She'd seen it. What had Oliver gone through in his last moments? It was too terrible to think about, but Diane couldn't help but think about it, and cried harder until no thoughts or fears filled her. Just the emptiness of a complete breakdown.

Time passed. She didn't know how much, but she eventually stopped crying and gave into more dry heaving, drool spilling off her lower lip and pooling on the cabin floor. "I need my stuff. I need to get this under control," she told herself aloud.

She went to her bag and unzipped her stash pocket, pulled out her jar of special stuff and her glass Cheshire Cat pipe. She carried them back to the bed and sat down, wiping her wet, hot face and dribbling nose. "Get it together, Diane," she said under her breath, angry at herself, and ticked at Lex for not checking on her even though she didn't want anyone to see her like this. Especially him.

She opened the lid of her jar. Reached in, looking down into it…where did half of it go?

She blinked. Her tears dried up. She'd brought a lot, knowing the stress of the trip might give her these kinds of stomach issues waking up. It looked like half of it was gone, and she hadn't yet touched it.

"What the hell?"

She dumped the jar out on the bunk, picked through the greenery as though what was left would have some clue as to where the rest of it went. Had she been sleepwalking last night? She did that too, sometimes. But she'd never sleep-*smoked*.

"Where'd it all go?"

Her stomach cramped hard and she felt dizzy. She hated feeling weak so much, and she gently slapped her cheek a couple times. She packed the pipe and smoked a couple puffs, and within minutes, her shoulders loosened up and her stomach settled.

She stayed there longer than she meant to. The escape was welcome right then. Her special smoke was missing, and that was a mystery. Oliver was dead, and that was a tragedy. The ship was going nowhere, and that was devastating. No way to contact the outside world for help.

They were stuck anchored at Aña Nuevo Island until god knew when with a shark who liked to chew its kills long and hard before they died, and then spit them out uneaten. Thrill killer. A real monster.

Her earlier irrational fear of them all falling prey to a giant great white shark's evil soul was no longer irrational.

It was real.

CHAPTER SIX

Chas had to keep busy. That was the only way he could cope. He ran over footage of the night before, between the hours when Oliver had been missing and everyone noticed. Even though some of their cameras had night vision, the storm was rough. And he only had a small part of the island to look at. Still, it was something. Something to do.

Chas glanced over at Bunny. She, too, was on a computer, but he couldn't see what she was up to. It didn't matter, really. He didn't bother starting up a conversation. Bunny wasn't a talker. Pretty as hell, but either shy or antisocial. Chas looked back to the list of footage files and picked a camera that had faced the west side of the inlet and a little bit of the island beyond, selected 2 am, and played the footage.

Sea lions and more sea lions. Who cared about the damn sea lions anymore? This trip had nothing whatsoever to do with their original research. Now it had to do with getting out of there.

They were scheduled to be finished and sailing the next day. Dr. Hammerstein made it clear to Chas before he left the workroom cabin that they probably weren't going anywhere for at least another day or two.

The storm was much worse than predicted.

Chas fast-forwarded the footage through the parts where the wind blew the rain into the camera, obscuring anything from being seen.

He put his chin on his fist, leaned into the monitor, and clicked away on his mouse.

At 3:08 am on the camera's footage, Chas stopped. He rewound. Played it, holding his breath. Rewound it again and watched in slow motion.

In the distance, beyond the sea lions' inlet, he could have sworn he saw two figures moving. One had its hands outstretched for a moment, which is what made the figures stand out to begin with. Otherwise, Chas would have thought they were more interference from the storm the night before.

He blinked, rubbed his eyes. Two? Oliver hadn't been alone?

"Bunny, hey," he said. "Hey, come over here and look at this."

Bunny stood up and came to him, brows furrowed, and looked over his shoulder. He pointed to the paused screen. "Watch right here." He wiggled his finger. "I'm going to play it slow-mo."

He hit play, and watched Bunny's usually impassive face focus, eyes widening. "People. Two people. Two people on the island." She looked down at him. "You found this on footage from last night?"

"Yeah. Yeah, I did." He had a hard time catching his breath.

"Play it again, please."

He did, watching the two figures again. The one holding its arms out for a moment. Then a gust of rain that wiped out any new images. Once the rain blew away, the figures were gone.

"Has to be Oliver," Bunny murmured. "But who's with him? That's two. Two people."

Chas thought for a minute. He knew where everyone had been at that time except for Oliver, Dr. Hammerstein. And Lex.

Lex had said he drank beer on the bridge instead of going to bed.

Had he?

Chas didn't want to say anything to Bunny. He had to think about this.

It didn't make any sense...unless Lex had been with Oliver, and not drinking beer.

But, what did all this mean? What were the implications if that was, indeed, Lex and Oliver walking the island at three in the morning in the raging sea storm? Lex...what did he know, saying it were him?

"It has to be Oliver, one of them," Bunny said quietly. "Who...the other?"

"Dunno," Chas mumbled, his brain whirling.

Lex was the only one who made sense, but Chas kept his mouth shut.

After a moment, he decided to go find Diane in her cabin. She hadn't come back since she'd gone to take care of her upset stomach, and deal with Oliver in her own way. She might still be in there.

"Bunny, I'll be back. Back up this file, admin lock it. Hide it." He stood up.

"Yeah. Yeah, okay. Where are you going?" She cocked her head at him, looking up into his eyes, worry in her own.

"I had a thought. I'm going to talk to D."

"Okay, sure." Bunny sat at Chas' desk and began working as he left. He went down the hall to the sleeping quarters.

He knocked on Diane's door. No answer. He knocked again, and called out, "Diane? It's Chas. You in there?"

"Yeah," came her muffled response. "Yeah. Hang on."

He heard her come to the door and then she opened it. She looked like hell. Her eyes were puffy like she'd done nothing but sob for the last hour. "Sorry," she said, seeing his concern at her appearance. "I just…it's… I had to do what Melody said. Process. I know how I look."

"It's okay. Don't worry about it." He smiled weakly at her. "Come on in."

Chas paused. "Is Lex here?"

"No."

"Where is he?"

"I don't know." She sounded peeved when she said it, so Chas didn't press the issue. He was glad Lex wasn't there.

He went in and sat on a wooden chair while Diane took the bottom bunk. Her good stuff was spread over the white sheets.

"What's all that for?" Chas asked, keeping his tone of voice as gentle as possible. He never thought of Diane as a softie, but rather a pillar of strength and progressiveness. Here she was, looking like she might never stop crying with weed all over her damn bed.

"It's the stuff I keep for when I wake up bad. You know, stomach."

"Yeah, yeah. But why…why is it all over your covers?"

As though she just noticed it, she started cleaning it up and putting bits back in her stash jar. "I came back here, you know, and got this for my stomach. But Chas, half of it is gone. I can't figure it out."

"Gone?" Chas was astounded. "Where did it go? Did you ask Lex about it? I mean, he might have smoked it."

"I haven't seen Lex." He voice sounded dead when she said it. Then, she added, "Besides, Lex never touches this. Nobody does. I mean, nobody, unless I offer."

Chas leaned forward in the cramped cabin and put his hand on her shoulder. "Someone did."

"Yeah. You're damn right they did." Anger burned her cheeks and her eyes watered, but not out of mourning.

"I know you want to be alone right now, but I just had a question or two for you. About Lex."

Diane met his stare. "What about Lex?"

"You said he wasn't here when Joseph and Melody brought you to bed last night. Do you remember him coming to bed?"

She looked down and shook her head. "No. I let go and went out. He was here when I woke up."

Chas paused, thinking, watching Diane go back to picking up crumbles of green and putting it in her jar. "Diane, was he awake?"

She stopped and looked at him again. "Yeah. He was reading. How did you know? Why did you ask that?"

He shook his head. The last thing he wanted to do was upset Diane with his suspicions about Lex, and where Lex could have been the night before instead of on the bridge. "I don't know," was all he could come up with. Chas wasn't much for keeping things to himself, but this? He knew he had to, though, until he could figure out what had happened, and if Lex was involved at all.

"He said he had a headache, a really bad one."

"Yeah? Reading what?"

"I can't remember now. I thought it was weird that he could still read with that bad of a headache. Well, he said it was awful, anyway."

Chas heard bitterness in her words. She was angry at Lex, probably because he wasn't there with her, comforting her. Chas could understand that.

And, why wasn't Lex doing just that? Where was he now?

"Okay, thanks, D. I'll let you get more rest."

"Chas," she said, eyes clear. "What do you know?"

"I don't know anything."

"You do. I can tell. What is it?"

"It's nothing. Nothing now. I'm trying to figure it out." Should he tell her about the footage? Sure, she had a weak time with hearing about Oliver, and then realizing they couldn't leave Aña Nuevo Island. Still, this was Diane. Tough as a bear, sharp as a chef's knife.

"Figure what out? Did you find something in the footage?"

"What do you mean?"

"I know you. You would have spent all this time looking at last night's footage. You wouldn't sit and cry like I did." She smiled slightly at him. "Tell me what you saw."

He wanted to, he really did. Diane was boss. She should know…but what if it were Lex, and if so, what did it mean?

Diane didn't need that worry. Chas wasn't going to give it to her, but he wouldn't hide the footage from her. "When you're feeling better, find Bunny. She'll show you what I found."

"Why won't you just tell me?" she pursued.

"Because I'm not sure what I saw. Like I said, I'm trying to figure it out. I promise, as soon as I know something, you'll be the first to know. Okay? Promise." He was desperate to get out of there because if Diane pushed a little more, he'd spill his worries. She didn't need that, not now.

Chas could handle this.

Thankfully, her watchful eyes relented, and she said, "Okay, thank you, Chas. I'll get myself together and see Bunny. I'll find you later."

He smiled at her, trying to lighten it up. "Not if I see you first."

*

Lex stood on the portside deck of the yacht in rain gear and soaked up the raging weather. He had a lot on his mind. He'd thought for sure Oliver's leg would have gotten washed out to sea. He hated that he didn't clean up. He always cleaned up, but Great White Death had scared him the night before, and he hadn't taken care of Oliver's leg.

Now, he would always have to have a bat body on him, and right then, he did. His inside pockets were full of them, and one was in the outside hand pocket of his raincoat. Somebody would put together that Lex and Oliver had both been officially unaccounted for at the same time last night.

After the reveal in the main cabin, Lex had slipped away when nobody noticed and had thrown four beers in the sea. He'd watched the wild currents take the cans far, far away. He had to make sure if anyone counted, beer was missing. Enough for Lex to have been gone for as long as he'd said he had been.

Now, he watched the rough sea beating the boat and island. Great White Death was near. Lex could almost feel him. It was like they were connected, but Lex couldn't understand it. He and that deadly shark were creating a true nightmare for normal people and enjoying it. He understood Great White Death.

He knew the shark cared nothing for this connection. Lex was a possible screaming victim.

Nightmare for normal people. Normal people like Oliver. Lex still felt the gloom of losing Oliver the night before now that he completely understood him. His mind raced with the wind and lightning.

He wished he still smoked. It would have been nice to have one right then, because Lex was stressed out. He didn't want to be around the others, especially Diane, because they would talk to him, ask him questions. Lex always had an answer, but they might all, right now, be figuring it out, putting together what Lex did, or at least that Lex knew something. They could be in a cabin, all together, scheming on how to confront him.

They weren't killers like Lex. But they would do something, like tie him up. Lex would slice them all to pieces before they revealed his core being to the world and he ended up in jail. That would be easy to explain when he could clean up and radio out for help once the ship's gear worked again, but the main problem was still there.

Lex hadn't had his chance to know Diane, save her, and then live a long, long happy life with her, knowing her completely, feeling the deepest love two people could share. The most intense love and devotion he would ever experience. He wanted it more than he'd ever desired anything, and that was the crux.

Lex couldn't take the obvious route and kill them all. He had to keep his inner killer a secret from Diane, and thus from everyone because of hiding it from her, and not rampage and take care of his mistake on the island the night before by slaughtering all of them one by one to cover his tracks.

His future with Diane was too important. It was the most important thing Lex had ever needed. And yes. He *needed* it.

He watched the mainland in the hazy distance, sometimes seeing it through the rain, sometimes not. They were so close to civilization, but this storm held them all captive. Even a flare or two would go completely unnoticed.

Lex didn't feel like a captive. He was grateful for this storm. It gave him more time. It gave him more of a chance to *know* Diane.

"Lex." He heard Chas coming up on his right. He looked at the techie, assessed him. So, they weren't all holed up plotting against him. That was good. Still, Lex could see in Chas' expression fear and uncertainty. The weak could not hide their weaknesses from Lex. Lex could see Chas had it figured out. He knew. He *knew* about Lex and Oliver.

Lex got all this in the way Chas said his name and the expression on his face in an instant. He reached his hand inside his pocket and palmed the bat body, sliding it out of its wrapping. "Hey, Chas."

"Hey, what are you doing out here in this storm?" Chas, too, looked at the dark shape of the mainland. Lex noticed his voice was tight. That meant he was nervous. Chas would be on alert. Lex had to be smooth, even as a seething rage filled him all over again that he'd not cleaned up.

Lex liked Chas, and he didn't want to kill him.

Still, this was a tricky game. He had to keep Chas from asking the questions he came to ask. Lex needed to distract him.

If his instinct that Great White Death was near was right, he could take care of Chas. He could do it now…and then it hit him.

It worked with Oliver.

Lex might get to know Chas completely, and soon.

"Chas," Lex started, making sure he had control over the conversation. "There's this one Great White Death story I've been thinking about."

Chas shook his head and wiped rainwater from his cheeks. "Not now, Lex. Don't you think enough is enough with that goddamn shark?" Anger in his voice. "I came to find you to tell you I found something on the footage. Oliver wasn't alone. I saw two figures from one of the camera feeds. Two."

"The shark, that's what I'm trying to tell you. I think it's a clue. A clue from an old legend." He waited, seeing if Chas would take the bait and drop whatever accusation he was about to make in the name of politeness.

The techie sighed, looked out to sea, then back at Lex. "Okay, a clue how?" Chas put his hands in his coat pockets, and Lex sensed Chas' frustration with not being able to confront Lex about whatever he knew right away. That was good. Lex now had the conversation.

He put his back against the rail of the boat and looked to the side at Chas. "Once, not too long ago, there was a 24-old man who came to Aña Nuevo Island during the stormy season. He was a researcher. Like us. He studied sea lions. He was very smart." Lex waited, watching Chas.

Chas kept his eyes on the mainland, and Lex saw his moment. He slid the bat body out of his pocket and put it behind his back.

"This guy was a lonely type. Not any good friends, not many who he could relate to. Maybe not anyone, ever, except for, say, his father growing up." Lex slipped his butterfly knife out with his other hand, palming it, until it was behind his back with the bat body.

Chas sighed. "Look, cut the crap and tell me the clue. I don't need another gory story. Now's not the time, get it?"

"I know, but you really need to hear it to understand the clue. No gore. No overdoing it for laughs and thrills. I know this is real. We all do. But to understand what I'm figuring out, you have to hear the way the legend goes."

Chas turned to him and Lex's hands froze behind his back. He angled his body so his hidden hands were facing the walkway of the side of the boat they stood on, and acted like he had complete focus on what Chas said next, like he really cared. He needed Chas to chill out enough for Lex to summon the great white shark. "What are you figuring out, Lex? Can't you just say it? Plainly?"

"It's about Oliver. It's about what I think happened."

Chas' expression changed slightly. Did Lex see fear? Definitely uncertainty. In a soft voice, almost not heard over the crack of thunder that hit, he said, "I think you know exactly what happened to Oliver."

That took Lex by surprise. He'd thought he had control of the situation. Now, he'd have to hurry this along. Chas wouldn't take his eyes off of Lex long enough for Lex to cut the bat body and toss it over, so he said, "Look. Look out over the sea."

Chas kept staring at him.

"No, for real. Look. That shark is out there. Somewhere, in all that deep, deep water, the killer lurks. That's the thing."

"I don't get it."

"You have to look. Look over the water. Go ahead," Lex urged. When Chas didn't do as told, Lex tried another tactic. "Chas, the shark scares me. We have to think like him before what happened to Oliver happens to all of us. Please, just look and listen."

Chas took a deep breath, broke eye contact, and looked at the sea.

Quick as the next flash of lightning, Lex slashed the bat body as he twisted his back to the rail, squeezed the blood, and dropped the bat into the depths.

Time was short now, and Lex's anticipation of knowing Chas made a thin layer of sweat rise up on his skin. It was going to happen, but he had to stay focused. Once Great White Death came, Lex was just as much of a target as Chas. If Lex's feeling of connection with the killer shark was right, the beast would be here at any moment.

"This guy, this smart researcher," Lex continued, stepping back from the rail and leaning against the wall behind it, "knew the legends of Great White Death. He'd seen him take out some smaller great whites earlier on the trip. He walked the island in hopes of catching a glimpse of the shark from the safety of land."

Chas looked down into the sea right before them.

"He thought the land was safe, but it's not. Nowhere is safe when this shark is around. Not me. Not you." Lex's breathing quickened at his own daring comment. He was toying with Chas, just waiting…waiting…excited, anxious.

"So, this guy got eaten. What's the lesson? What do you get from this?" Chas said, and his expression was wary.

Lex slipped the butterfly knife into his pocket. He looked away from Chas and to the water, and saw it. Lex saw the fin, a little bit away, but coming fast. Quickly, he said, "Look at me now. Right now. This is important."

Chas turned away from the railing and faced Lex, folding his arms across his chest. "Lex, I know you went with Oliver to the island last night. I saw footage of two people. It couldn't have been anyone other than you with Oliver. What the fuck do you—?"

Great White Death's gargantuan maw flung out of the sea, right toward Chas' back, and before Chas could finish his sentence, the giant killer shark snatched him by the head and flipped Chas backward into the water.

Lex's heart pumped so hard he thought it might fail. He couldn't miss this, hearing Chas, seeing it...but the shark wouldn't disappear after he'd had his way with the lead tech. Great White Death would come for Lex, and as soon as Chas expired.

Lex ran to the railing and bent over it.

Chas bobbed to the surface of the rough sea, screaming as soon as he had air in his lungs. Long, guttural howls. He had been scalped by the shark raking his teeth against Chas' head, and just red matter covered the top of his head as he flailed in the water.

Lex listened, tense. Chas wasn't quite there yet, but neither was Great White Death.

The shark surfaced his nose and eyes beside Chas, and then teeth, and nipped off one of Chas' arms with a quick bite and jerk. Blood spurted out of his arm socket, and then the real screaming started as Chas' eyes bulged in horror and from insane amounts of pain.

Great White Death submerged, and must have grabbed one of Chas' legs, because Chas swooped under the surface in an instant.

Lex had just started to hear it…hear Chas… Great White Death wouldn't let him down. He was sure of it. The shark wanted the screams as badly as Lex did.

Lex was right. Chas resurfaced, belly up, missing now a leg. His mouth seemed ten times bigger than his scalped head, eyes closed, and he wailed all the pain in the world as the great white nibbled his ribs with his front teeth. The frothing, wild sea filled with dark, dark blood, so much.

And Chas cried out harder, louder, crazier.

He senses the spring coming, and is renewed of the dark of winter from its hope… Matter changes into new matter… Everything evolves into something else, old and new…

Great White Death wasn't getting enough satisfaction with the nips, and brought three especially gnarly, long front teeth down on Chas' stomach, puncturing Chas. He let out a choking sound and widened his eyes as his innards spilled out of him and into the sea.

"What the hell!" Lex heard Melody scream from down the deck. He paid no attention. He was listening to Chas.

Melody needed to shut the hell up.

Chas' intestines floated into the only hand he had left, and he fisted his fingers around them. There was nothing but right now and the horrid end in Chas' gaping, hollow eyes, gazing at the rain pounding his ripped face. Then he screamed again, still alive somehow with his insides all gushing out.

Action calls and he answers… Everything must be taken care of… That was the way of love… That was the way of change…

Melody ran up to Lex and grabbed his arm. "Goddamn it, Lex, what the fuck! Chas! Come on, Lex, come on." She tugged his arm, but Lex was in ecstasy. He heard so much more than that, he heard it all, everything that was Chas, that now had been Chas, and he was stunned and moved by how magnificent the man had been. Not just a techie, but a true warrior and hero.

"Come the fuck on! It went under, it's coming for us, you know it. Come on!" Melody cried out, desperately pulling on the front of Lex's jacket. "Move! Snap out of it!"

It was too late. The fin popped out of the water, back from the boat... and Lex knew that was on purpose. Great White Death had backed up so he could ram the boat.

It all happened so fast. The shark spun out of the water, its massive head ramming the rail Lex had been leaning on moments ago, and the yacht tipped over all the way to one side. Lex and Melody fell, rolling down the side of the ship against the wall. Lex heard people inside the boat screaming in horror and shock.

Diane.

He was already feeling the loss of Chas, which had stunned him from moving away from the rail, away from tempting the shark, but the impact took care of him. He and Melody landed in a heap at the back of the yacht, and, of course, Great White Death was not satisfied. There were more to slaughter, more on this manmade floating device to maul to pieces.

The shark went under, and almost immediately, slammed the top of his head into the hull of the yacht. It once seemed the safe place, where nothing could touch them, but now, the boat started sinking as it took on water down below. The metal screamed as the other side of the boat crunched into the rock of the island.

Lex had to get off the boat, now. All feelings of thrill and loss left him for the need to survive. He even forgot Diane, and scrambled to the other side of the tilting yacht, Melody right behind him. This side of the boat faced the island, with the yacht angled from the shark's repeated attacks on the hull. All Lex had to do was roll off the deck and onto the hard earth of the island, and then run.

And that's exactly what he did without looking back until he was so far inland that Great White Death couldn't possibly reach him. He stopped, bent over, heaving for breath like he was dying, and then whipped around. Melody was a few feet away from him, collapsed on the ground. Lex looked to the boat and remembered Diane. His love. His life. His true meaning.

"Diane!" he yelled.

Melody started yelling names, too.

The boat was sinking so fast, but to Lex's relief, he saw figures flying out of windows and doors onto the island, and they hit the ground running. Above it all, Great White Death's dorsal fin rose from the water, high above the now mostly submerged yacht, and rammed it one more time. Steel screeched, and the entire boat collapsed on itself, instantly sinking. It was gone as though it had never been.

Lex strained his watering eyes. Diane. How could he have left her? He squinted at the people running toward him, but couldn't make out who they were in the storm. "Diane!" he called out. "Diane!"

"Lex!" He heard her desperate answer through the rainfall's rage.

He sunk to the ground on his knees, holding out his arms, waiting for her. She made it. She was coming. He hadn't lost her. He hadn't lost her to the shark, and he never, ever would.

She fell into him and they rolled to the wet earth in each other's arms. She smelled so good, spicy and sweet. He had her. She sobbed into his hair, grabbing the roots of his curls in a death grip, and whispered, "I thought I lost you. Lex, oh. I thought the screams… I thought it was you…"

He stroked her soaked head. "Shh. It's okay, you're safe. We're safe. Shh. It's okay," he said into her ear, hoping his breath warmed her soul.

"Look," he heard Melody yell with a gasp. Diane jerked out of his grasp and turned to see what Melody was screaming about.

Lex sat up and looked.

Dr. Hammerstein, Aaron, Joseph, and Bunny were nearby, all watching where the boat had been, too.

The giant great white killer shark had driven up on the beach there, his head writhing back and forth on the reef, mouth opening and clamping shut, sounding like a bulldozer doing its job on a condemned house.

"Why won't it just go away?" Melody cried out.

Lex stood up, reaching down for Diane's hand. "It can't touch us here," he said. "We're all safe."

"Chas," Diane said.

Melody began crying, covering her eyes and bending over. "Oh, God. Chas. Chas, sweet, sweet Chas. I saw it. I saw it!"

Lex let his attention on the remaining crew and their shock fade away. He simply stared at the shark. How long could it be out of water like that, just gnashing teeth at empty air? Lex knew, though. Lex knew Great White Death was letting them all know what was in store for them, and that he would be hunting eternally from now on until they were all his.

CHAPTER SEVEN

Melody watched her best friend and roommate creating a fire pit in the lighthouse keeper's home they'd taken shelter in. Diane had used the old stove and broken furniture. Dr. Hammerstein was the only one whose lighter had made it from the boat and their run through the rain in working condition.

Nobody had spoken about Chas. As soon as they'd gotten in the lighthouse keep, Aaron, Lex, and Joseph were making plans to go back to where the boat crumbled and sunk to see if they could find anything left. Food? Medicines? Anything at all?

Aaron didn't want to go back so soon, especially after the shark's strange and terrifying display of attacking the air where they had been after the boat sunk. Melody agreed with him. That shark could be lying in wait for people to return. Still, she said nothing and kept her focus on Diane creating heat to dry them all off, get light in the musty, broken house.

Lex explained that the shark would have expended all its energy in such a violent and active attack, and would have retreated by then to gather strength and feed.

Feed, Melody thought. The thing didn't even eat Chas. It murdered him for the sake of doing so. What did it actually eat in those deep waters?

A chill raced through her wet body, and she sat close to the broken stove with its weak flame. She watched Diane continue to break chairs and tables, adding them to the firepit.

Why couldn't Melody do a goddamn thing? She was stuck. She guessed it was shock, guessed they all were in shock, and this is how they handled it, each in their own ways.

She had a feeling…that the shark would get her, get them all, like in Lex's stupid stories. She was being an idiot by even allowing herself to acknowledge it, but there it was.

Bunny came over and sat next to Melody, also quiet and watching Diane.

Dr. Hammerstein backed Lex's argument. He said if anything was to be salvaged, now was the only time they'd have a chance. Within an hour, anything that might have made it would have washed out to sea in the wild currents of the storm.

"Aaron, you don't have to go. Just me and Lex can get it," Joseph told him.

"I'm going, too," Dr. Hammerstein insisted. "I'm not that old, so don't start."

"No, man," Aaron said. "You guys know your sharks. I have to go. We need as many hands as possible in case there's a lot of wreckage we can bring back. We only got one shot at this."

Lex walked over to Diane and she stood straight from fanning a flame, looking up at him. He put his hand on her cheek. "Thanks, Diane, for starting the fire. Don't worry. We'll be fine. We're going now." He leaned into her and gently kissed her lips. She barely closed her glazed eyes.

"Watch the water at all times. Someone be a lookout," Diane said to Lex.

"Yes, excellent idea, Diane," Dr. Hammerstein told her. "Aaron, that's what you can do while the three of us scour the beach."

Melody zoned out for a little bit then. Overstimulated, she called it to herself. Overstimulated was when everything was too much and she left reality for a spell. She was barely aware when the men went out, and kept her gaze on the growing, warm flames.

She came out of her trance when Bunny took off her sweater. She wore a loose black T-shirt underneath. "Diane, it's great. I'm warming up," Bunny said.

Melody realized she was, too, but there was ice deep in her heart that no fire could melt. "I'm sorry."

Diane dropped a pile of broken furniture next to the firepit. "Melody? Why?"

She met Diane's concerned eyes. "I should have helped you make the fire. I'm sorry. I just sat here." She looked down.

"Why don't you sit and rest, Diane?" Bunny suggested.

Diane didn't need to be cajoled into it, and sat between Bunny and Melody. She put her face in her palms. "Oh God, that was awful. This is all so, so awful." She reached out and put her hand on Melody's upper arm. "You never apologize to me for that again. We all did what we had to do after that. I needed to do something, and you needed to go zen. That's what you do, and you know it's okay."

"Yeah," Bunny said in her light, soft voice. "I feel so helpless. But maybe, Melody, you and I needed to let it all sink in. I know you'll be fine in no time."

Bunny had never said anything even somewhat personal to Melody, and she looked at the young tech.

"Thanks, Bunny. Thanks." She smiled slightly. "Fuck."

"That's right, fuck," Diane answered.

The three of them were quiet for a while as they watched the fire, felt the warmth. A feeling of safety came over Melody, like the rain had stopped and the sun had come out. It was all going to be okay. They'd stick together. They'd weather the storm.

Melody had her cell, and even if it had no signal now, once the storm cleared, they'd be out of there in no time.

"Right. Absolutely," she told the other two.

"What?" Diane asked, cocking her head at Melody. Her hair was half dry, hanging in blonde kinks.

"Sorry, was thinking to myself and then answering out loud." She patted Diane's arm. "Bunny, you're right. You're so quiet, but you watch. You probably know all of us better than we know ourselves. I am better. I'm much better. We stay here. They'll find some supplies. They've been gone a while. That means they're getting stuff. See?" She pulled her cell out of her coat pocket. "Waterproof case. I charged it and turned it off the night we lost signal. Storm'll break in a day or two, and we can call out. Rescue. Nobody else will get hurt."

Bunny nodded at Melody. Her usual noncommittal response to a comment directed to her. Who was Bunny, really? Melody always had liked her, but didn't give her much thought. Now, she felt close to her. A survivor thing? Probably. She'd take it.

"You two," Melody continued, "you know we're fine. Nobody goes near the water. We stay in this house until my phone says go."

"Yes," Diane said. "That's how we do it. That's how we get through this. Together, alive, with our brains." She turned to Melody again. "What happened to you? When the shark hit?"

They didn't know anything about Chas except Lex letting them know he was gone, taken by the great white.

Melody didn't want to think about what she saw when she got on deck earlier, how she'd watched Lex and Chas talking, and then...and then...

She closed her eyes. "I was on the deck where Chas and Lex were. I was there when the shark got Chas, and then rammed the boat." Her own voice sounded dead to her ears. She had to just get the facts out to answer the question and wanted to leave it there. She redirected back to Diane. "You? Where were you?" She leaned forward and looked at Bunny. "You, too. How did you all get out?"

Bunny and Diane exchanged a look. "We were together in the main cabin. When the boat rocked over, all the windows smashed out. Bunny and I jumped out and rolled. We could hear Chas..." She trailed off.

"What were you two doing?" Melody asked.

"Well, Chas came to talk to me before. I mean, after I went to my cabin. He asked questions about Lex. He told me to ask Bunny to show me footage Chas found from last night when Oliver was missing."

"What? What was it?" Melody asked.

"You could see two people in the distance from one of the beach line cameras. The storm had too much interference, and you could only see them for a minute, but it was two people. Had to have been."

"Two? Oliver wasn't alone?"

Diane shook her head, eyes dead serious with the implications.

Bunny said it. "Someone with us is lying, hiding something."

Melody and Diane looked at Bunny. "What? You mean, someone was with Oliver, and when he was missing, didn't say anything? No way. We all have known each other for, like, six years."

Bunny's gaze never wavered.

Diane said, "Could there be someone else on the island?"

That scared the crap out of Melody. "Some weirdo? What? That's freaky. And why in the world would Oliver go out on the island and hang out with this dude? I mean, what were they doing in the footage?"

"It was hard to tell. One of them held his arms out and dropped them really fast. That's kind of how you notice them. They're so far away. I wish you could have seen it," Bunny said. "I know you would have figured something out from seeing it that we didn't."

"Someone else on the island," Melody murmured. "This island is off-limits to anyone other than researchers with permits. I mean, if there's one person, couldn't there be more? I mean, this island is tiny, though. Right? We would have seen someone."

"We hadn't been in here," Diane said. "In this house."

Melody waved her arms around. "This house is dead. The walls are knocked out mostly. I can see upstairs through the broken ceiling. Nobody's here." She dropped her voice. "Are they?"

"If they were, they aren't anymore," Diane answered.

"Guys," Bunny said, her hands clasped together so tightly that her knuckles were white. "You didn't hear me. There's nobody on the island but us."

"What? You mean what you said about someone hiding something?" Melody asked her. "Someone on our team?"

"There's more to this, there has to be," said Bunny, but she did that thing where she stopped making eye contact and watched her clenched hands. "I don't know. Never mind."

Diane turned to Melody. "Think. Did you see anything else when you found Lex and Chas? Right before the shark came?"

"Lex had his butterfly knife out. Yeah. He slid it in his pocket right before the thing came." Melody surprised herself by remembering that detail.

"Why would he have his knife out?" Diane asked. She answered herself. "Well, Lex does like to do tricks with it. Absent-minded habit when he wants a cigarette. Maybe that's what he was doing."

"In the rain?" Melody said.

Diane shrugged. "Lex is weird. Good weird, but weird."

They were interrupted by the guys' return, Aaron coming in first, carrying a duffel. "The guns!" he said. "They were wedged in some rocks of the reef. Got the harpoon, too."

Lex appeared next. Diane got up and went to him. "Everything was okay? You're all safe? No shark?"

Lex hugged her after he put down two coolers and a stack of wet blankets. "No shark. We got some stuff." He gestured at Dr. Hammerstein and Joseph as they came inside with more plunder from the wreckage. "They even found some canned food."

Bunny's quiet voice by the fire said, "Good thing you have your butterfly knife."

Melody whipped her head to Bunny. What did that mean?

"What?" Lex said, staring at Bunny.

"Your knife. The one you always have. You can open the cans."

Was it Melody's imagination, or did Lex smile too easily? Maybe easily wasn't the right way to put it, but considering their situation, and Chas and Oliver's horrible deaths, Lex almost seemed too casual.

"That's right. Let me check..." He reached in his pocket and pulled out the knife. "Yep, it made it."

"Good," Diane said, and bent to a small metal cooler with a lock. "Your champagne?"

"Yeah," Lex said. "It's the weirdest thing."

"I don't know about you, but I never want to drink champagne again," Aaron said, wiping rainwater from his face with his soaked sleeve.

"Me neither," Lex added.

Yes, Melody thought. *Too casual was more like it.* Was this Lex's way of handling shock? To ignore it, to give off the vibe that everything was under control?

Come to think of it, Melody realized, Lex always seemed to enjoy control. Not in a maniacal, crazy-CEO-making-everyone-slaves kind of way, but he kept cool. Composed. He could hold them all spellbound when he told one of his shark legends, no matter how long it was, and she knew he loved doing that.

Still, through something like this? They all showed cracks of strain, from the ways they held their bodies to the tension in their tones of voices.

Lex seemed normal, but there was sadness, too.

Melody didn't think Lex was sad about the same things everyone else was, and her seed of suspicion was planted in that moment. It was despair and depression sadness she picked up on, not hysteria and madness. He had an air of keeping appearances, but Melody could tell he wasn't good.

She was being ridiculous. It was stupid Lex. What was she thinking? He wasn't the other figure with Oliver. Bunny wasn't right about one of their group hiding something...and it wouldn't be Lex. No way.

Even as Melody forced herself to dismiss the thought and get to helping sort through the loot from the sunken boat, she was well-aware of said seed having been planted. At that moment, she'd let it gestate, and put it aside.

There was just too much to deal with right now.

*

Melody was usually a picky eater, choosing starving over anything veggie, but she devoured her can of French-cut green beans that night as they sat around the fire with each of their own canned goods. Lex's butterfly knife had, indeed, come in handy in opening the food.

There wasn't much conversation. Diane and Lex were off to the side in deep conversation. He had his arm around her, stroking her hair as she rested her head on his shoulder and ate her corn slowly with her fingers. They had no silverware. All of them used their digits as forks.

Bunny was in a corner on her side, and Melody assumed she was asleep. Dr. Hammerstein and Joseph talked in low tones about shark behavior. Aaron sat next to Melody, trying to cheer her up, she supposed. He talked about a bunch of nothing, but it was a nice distraction.

"When we get home," he was saying, "I'm getting a steak. A strip. No, a T-bone. That's right. You'll go with me. We can get one of each."

"Then Mexican after," Melody added, keeping it light.

"With huge margaritas."

"The kinds with the beer dumped upside-down in them."

"That's right. As much as I said I could never drink champagne again, I sure as hell could go for it now. Anything. There's no way I'll be able to sleep."

"Me neither," Melody said, glancing over at Lex and Diane. Lex still had that coolness about him. It didn't feel right to her, and who else could have been on the beach with Oliver other than Lex?

But if that were true, then why wouldn't Lex have told them what happened?

That wasn't like Lex, unless seeing Oliver's death kind of broke some part of his soul. That could be it, but she doubted it. The seed's fruit was breaching the surface of the soil of her subconscious, seeking light.

"Hey Lex," Aaron called over to him in a soft voice. "What about that champagne, man?"

Lex patted Diane's arm and she sat up. "Yeah," Diane said. "That might be good. We could sleep. I mean, other than Bunny, who the hell is going to get a bit of sleep? Not me. Lex?" She looked over at him with a slight smile.

He took his arm from around Diane. "Let me see…" He fumbled in his jeans' pockets, then pulled his hands out, empty. "I don't have the key. It must have been onboard. I honestly can't remember where I put it."

"Damn," said Aaron.

"Yeah, damn," said Diane. Melody noticed she had that look, the one she got before she crashed out and slept hard for 20 minutes. Her blue eyes crossed slightly and her head bobbed.

It had taken Melody a couple years to see the signs because Diane hid it so well. Melody wasn't an idiot, and she *was* a snoop. She'd found Diane's narcolepsy pills a long time ago during their third year living together as undergrads.

No, Melody wasn't an idiot. She knew the implications of Diane's schooling and career path if that was known. She'd never brought up to Diane that she knew, nor had she told a living soul.

"We can break the lock," Melody said. "Right, D? Lex?"

Lex shook his head, looking down. "I wish. That sucker is titanium. No clue how to just break it."

"Break the damn cooler," said Aaron.

Diane leaned over onto her elbow, hand propping up her head. Melody could tell she was fighting that odd sleep with everything she had. "We'd smash the champagne."

"Yeah," Lex said. "I think it's a bust. Too bad some beer didn't wash up from the wreck. I know I could use something for my nerves."

Melody eyed him. "You don't even seem shook up. You're...sad, I guess. But you're doing the best of all of us."

"He has to stay strong for me," Diane said with a wink at Lex.

"It's the other way around," Lex said, grinning back at Diane. "I have to save face and keep up with her attitude."

"You two make me sick," Melody said lightly, hiding her concern for Diane, trying to think of some way to wake her up. Then again, it might be nice for her to be blissfully unconscious. Still, Melody saw Diane pulling the hair on her upper arm, and that was a sign Melody knew meant Diane was trying to stay awake.

She patted Aaron on the shoulder. "I'm going to take over." She stood up and walked over to Diane and Lex. "You, Lex. Take a break and finally get all the way dry by the fire. Some of these blankets are pretty much dry, too. Maybe when you come back, get one for D?"

Lex smiled at her. "Yeah, good thinking. I'm pretty cold, actually. Diane, want that blanket now?"

"In a minute. You go ahead."

He got up and sat next to Aaron by the fire, and they began talking quietly.

"You okay?" Melody said to Diane.

"Yeah, of course. Well, no, but, you know. I'm okay," Diane said, eyes drooping.

"Is there anything I can do?"

She smiled. "Why all the concern? I've been over here worried to death about you. You're hardly talking and you ate green beans. Are *you* okay?"

Melody shook her head. "You know I'm a mess. I mean…never mind."

"Now you sound like Bunny," Diane teased.

Melody shrugged. "I can't get the image out of my head, the sounds. Chas. You know?" She said it quietly so only Diane could hear. Her friend's eyes softened and she got her focus back. The sleepiness was staved off for a moment, Melody saw.

"I can't imagine how horrible it must have been for you." She reached out and touched Melody's bent knee. "Just knowing is killing me. Oliver, Chas. That thing in the sea. But you saw it." She closed her eyes for a moment, and then opened them, watching the fire. "I've been dreaming. Ever since we saw the great white attack those baby sharks. Nightmares."

"Really?"

"Every time I sleep, just about. I'm the one who gets eaten from back to front."

"That sounds just awful. You sleep so much. You're having this nightmare a lot, you said. Even with your naps?"

"Yeah, yeah. I hate it. Makes me never want to sleep again."

Melody knew that feeling as the memory of scalped Chas in the water, unrecognizable, flashed through her mind.

She needed to know where Diane stood now that she'd had time to think about the footage. The timing of how it could only be Lex with Oliver on the island the night before. The couple had seemed like nothing had changed, but Melody knew Diane wouldn't change a thing until she was sure about something.

This meant she wasn't sure. It was a sensitive subject, but Melody had to bring it up. "Diane, have you thought more about Oliver? The footage?"

Diane stopped smiling and didn't look at Melody for a moment. Melody waited impatiently, but she didn't push.

Finally, Diane whispered, "If there is nobody else on the island, it was Dr. Hammerstein or Lex." Her eyes slid over to meet Melody's. "Mel, I don't think it was Dr. Hammerstein." Diane's face was a steel mask and Melody couldn't tell a thing about what Diane was trying to say.

"What?"

"What do you mean, what?"

Melody leaned into Diane. "I think it was Lex, too," she whispered.

Diane closed her eyes and rubbed her temple with her free hand. "It's the only thing that makes sense, and it makes no sense at all at the same time."

"Unless…"

"Yeah, unless there's something very strange going on with Lex. Right, Melody?" Diane sounded pissed and it took Melody aback. Diane never got angry.

She didn't know how to respond, so she brought up one of her ideas. "If he was with Oliver, he could have seen something that disturbed him so much that he can't deal."

"Maybe," Diane said. "That would explain the change in his behavior and why he didn't tell anyone about it, acted like he had no clue where Oliver was this morning. I guess it's possible he blocked it out or something crazy like that." She rubbed her whole face then. "But to be honest, I don't think that's it."

"What do you think, then?"

Diane sat up and looked Melody dead in the eye. "I love Lex. You know that."

"You told me he's the one and only."

She paused with a horribly intense look on her face. "But on this trip, Lex isn't acting like the Lex I know." She barely said the words, she was so quiet.

"What do you mean?"

"I mean, well, like I said. I love Lex. I love the Lex I know, the one we all know, but what if...?"

"What if what?"

Diane started to whisper something else, but looked up. "Oh, thanks!"

Melody turned. Lex was behind her with dry blankets for both of them. "Here you go, ladies. Diane, I thought you might be getting tired, and Melody, you need to try resting. We all do. I already talked to the others, but I'm going to stay awake until around four, and then wake up Joseph to stand watch and sleep myself."

"Watch for what?" Diane asked. If Melody hadn't just heard Diane's suspicions, she'd think D was being her usual loving self to Lex.

"Anything. Anything at all. Someone needs to be awake at all times."

"The shark can't get us here," Diane said. "That's just impossible."

Lex nodded. "I know, but Joseph and I feel the same way about it. Here." He handed them the blankets, bent down and gave Diane a kiss, and added, "Go on, snuggle up, you two. You'll help each other relax. Cuddle up like kittens."

"Ha," Diane said, lying down and wrapping the blanket around her. "Come on, Mel. Spoon me."

Melody laid down on the hardwood floor and tucked the blanket around her. "I prefer to be the spoonee so we're gonna have to settle for face-to-face."

"Sounds perfect," Diane said, and her eyes got that unfocused look again, and fast.

"Love you," Lex told Diane.

"Love you, too."

Diane was asleep before Lex had reached the front door to the keep, where Melody assumed he planned to keep watch. There was no way Melody was sleeping. Hell no. Not after what she'd seen, and not after what Diane herself said about Lex.

Lex might be watching the sea, but Melody was going to watch Lex.

*

Lex sat on the wood floor just inside the keep's front doorway, looking out at the black storm. He couldn't even see the water, but he heard it between thunderclaps, and caught glimpses of white, cresting waves in the flashes of lightning.

He was thinking about Melody, feeling her eyes on him.

She was on to him. He knew it. She at least had suspicions. Had she seen the footage Chas had told him about? Did she know everything Chas had?

Lex had to assume she did. He wasn't going to underestimate her, or anyone, for that matter.

It was just so hard right now. The loss of Chas from his life was devastating, and it was more difficult than usual for Lex to keep his head on straight after a *knowing*. He heard Chas, heard who he was, and knew him completely.

This shark business was different than killing them himself. There was no regret to temper the loss. Just pure, empty loss. Lex couldn't have stopped Great White Death with Chas.

He needed to plan on how to do it right with Diane, he had to take care of Melody, keep the others from being suspicious. Right now, though, the complete and utter crushing depression was fogging his mind.

Think, he told himself. He could truly mourn Chas later. Yes. He needed to figure out his priorities. Right now, Melody seemed like the only suspicious one in the group. That meant she had to go.

Lex frowned at the darkness outside. Melody was Diane's best friend. It would devastate her if Melody died. Lex didn't want to do that to Diane.

Then, it hit him. He put together the sadness without regret with Melody's death not being his fault if he were to, say, lead her out onto the island, somewhere near the water.

He reached in his coat and felt for a bat body. It was stiff. He cursed in his head. He'd have to get to the cooler and get a fresh one. All of the bat bodies were like the first, he saw as he felt through the stash in his coat. How could he open the cooler with Melody's ever-watchful eye on him?

Another thought occurred to him, lifting his low spirits. If he possibly could get Melody to the water, and lure Great White Death to her, he could practice saving her like he planned to do with Diane.

A shiver went down his spine. To do that, he'd have to be right there in the action. Was he ready to risk that? It seemed something only to risk for the real prize, not as practice. The legendary, cursed shark would do everything it could to keep Melody and take Lex, too. Was this worth the risk?

He gave it more thought, and then he realized it could happen yet again. Again! He could *know* Melody. Know her core being, her everything. What Lex lived for, what he killed for.

His sadness lightened at the prospect. The idea of having it again, twice in one day, was so tantalizing that the passing thought of losing her after (because she had to go in the end), and the depression that would follow, didn't deter him. It was worse not to *know* than it was to live without them afterward, that is, when the opportunity and need arose. Right now, he had both, but first, he had to figure out how to get into the cooler.

He had an idea.

Lex stood up, stretched lazily for show even though he was as wired as an LED bulb, and slowly turned around. Yep, Melody was staring right at him. "Can't sleep, Melody?" he asked quietly.

"No," she whispered. "What are you doing?"

"I'm going to take this cooler up to some rocks in the middle of the island and try to break it open. I could use a goddamn drink. You want some champagne if I get it?" He smiled at her.

She smiled back, but he could tell it was fake. She had an idea he was with Oliver, probably had made up her mind about it, and wasn't sleeping because she wanted to keep watch on him. "Sure, yeah. And hey, good luck with that. Why don't you stick close to the house? That's stupid. There's something in this house you can break that cooler lock with."

"Maybe I can get a piece of pipe from some old plumbing outside of the house. Maybe from behind the bathroom. You think?" He raised his eyebrows.

"Probably. Sounds like a plan."

"Then, that's what I'll do."

"You're seriously going out there?"

"Yeah."

"Are you nuts?" Melody propped up on an elbow as Lex crossed the room to the cooler.

Before he bent to pick it up, he looked at her, letting some of his sadness come to the surface, but just for a moment. He'd already started sweating from thinking about knowing Melody.

It was going to happen.

"I'm having a hard time with all of this." He quickly looked down and picked up the cooler. "Alright, alright. Going to find a hard pipe. I'll be back."

He left quickly. He hoped to entice her to confront him like Chas had, but he'd need to be by the water. As he left, he exuded mystery with his physical form, shoulders hunching, head down. He even flipped his coat hood up right at the last minute like he hid a deformity from prying eyes.

It went something like that.

Melody would follow.

He walked slowly through the storm, not out of methodical planning or plotting, but he couldn't see but when the lightning came, and there was no way he was risking walking right up on the water.

The shark knew him now. He'd seen Lex three times. He wouldn't forget. When Lex knew victims personally, the *knowing* was more intense and pleasurable. It must be the same for Great White Death.

*

Lex sat on the bat cooler—which actually was a heated, chemical cooler to keep the bodies limp and fresh for a few days—by ocean's edge on a large, smooth rock. His hands trembled as he turned the bat body over and over in his hands. He couldn't bring himself to unwrap it. Great White Death knew him. Knew he had the bats. It hadn't occurred to him until he was getting ready for Melody.

He heard her Converse scuff the drenched rock as she climbed up behind him.

"Hello, Melody," he said without looking at her, and his fear left. Anticipation filled him. He unwrapped the bat body, palmed it with his knife, and looked over his shoulder through the rain at her.

Lightning flashed, and he saw her face completely. He knew her so well already. How would this go?

A sharp pain of sadness hit him, thinking of Oliver and Chas, and soon, Melody. Because even if he could save her, he'd have to kill her to keep his secret. The loss...the ecstasy. The balance in between was the hunt itself. He'd created this balance for himself.

"Hey, Lex," she said above the wind and thunder. "What the hell are you doing out here? You're right next to the water. Have you lost your mind?" She stayed back on the rock. That was no good. He needed her in front of him so that the shark would grab her, and he'd be close enough to grab her hands.

If Great White Death didn't flip her like Chas.

He half smiled at her, but she couldn't see it. His heart pounded louder in his ears than the storm around him. "Maybe I have," he said quietly.

"What?"

"Maybe I have."

She shook her head. "I can't hear you over this damn storm and there's no way in hell I'm coming any closer. Look," she said, her voice strong. Too strong. Lex could see she was forcing it so she'd feel on top of the power.

He had to make this happen fast. He turned away and did his thing with the bat. She wouldn't be able to see, so he didn't make much effort to be slick. He tossed the drained body to the black water.

"Look," she repeated. "What's going on? It's one of two things. You somehow broke when you saw Oliver get killed. We all know you were with Oliver."

So, they did all know. Diane. Diane knew.

He turned back to her and stood up.

He couldn't kill Melody. Diane would know for sure, then. She'd know everything. She knew he was with Oliver. Melody had given him an out. Yes, he could be "broken," could tell of his and Oliver's bonding on the beach. Tell Melody that, then all of them.

"Melody, you have to listen to me." He held a hand out and picked up the cooler, ran right for her. "The shark, it's coming. Come on." He grabbed her elbow and tried to shove her down off the smooth rock, but she must have tensed up when he ran at her, because Melody didn't budge.

Lightning lightened her face again. Lex saw wide, amber eyes full of surprise and fear. *She had no idea*, he thought. He looked at the water.

"That's it? You have this crazy thing going on in your head with this shark? Shark's not here all of a sudden. What's going on?" She yanked her arm away. "Why the fuck are you out here?"

Over the thunder, he heard the water break, a crash that only meant high-speed in or out of water, and something big. It was too late.

He spun around, grabbed Melody by her shoulders, and shoved her in front of him—right into Great White Death's ragged, giant killer teeth. The shark's mouth filled the air all around, it seemed, and Lex wasn't sure if he, too, was going in with Melody. In there, in those teeth that take their sweet time for thrills.

The shark's lower jaw scraped across the rock, slowing it down a little. Lex gave Melody a shove and pushed himself off her back to get out of the way.

His game was on again. He would have to save Melody, and not just for practice.

She wouldn't remember much about this. The shove was fine.

Great White Death snapped her up by the calves and feet, slopping her onto her back, her head cracking on the rock. She let out a yelp. The shark clamped his teeth down over her lower legs, and swung its head back and forth in a frenzy, dragging now-wailing Melody across the rock.

Lex was frozen. He was so close to him. To Great White Death. He saw how the shark's eyes didn't roll back as it attacked Melody, like it wanted to watch. This shark wasn't feeding, no.

He shook himself all over and ran into the chaos even as the ecstasy began. Melody was quick to get there with her death cries, but as Lex came up on her, slid on his belly toward her as she swung back around, he saw that from below her right knee, there was no limb. Not anymore, and black blood sprayed the shark's white teeth in splatters in the lightning. Melody was fast, but the shark was also killing faster.

She smells the sadness in the rose water... she drinks it so no one else might... find her, he will find her and forever happens...

The shark knew him. The shark wanted him. Not her.

He grabbed for her right hand and held onto a notch in the rock with his free hand. He caught her cramping claw and held on for everything he believed in and loved. Right then, he loved Melody so very much.

Great White Death had to take her other foot, because Lex didn't let go for anything. The screaming stopped, and Melody's eyes rolled up at his face. Black eyes. She was so beautiful, so good. So pale. "Help me..."

He snapped out of it and pulled what was left of her into his arms, standing swiftly as Great White Death slipped back into the water.

That was about five minutes of no water. Was that how long the shark could go without breathing?

Lex squeezed Melody to him, pressing her face into the crook of his neck. "I have you, I have you. You're okay," he screamed as he leapt off the rock, hearing the giant, murdering shark crashing down on the smooth stone behind him so hard it moved a little.

He slipped, of all things. His mind went blank, and he went into instinct mode. He used Melody's weight in front of him to pull them over the edge, and down they went, face-first.

Lex felt Melody's blood spill all over his right side. No, she couldn't die. Diane, she needed Melody. Melody was very important. There was so much about her he'd never thought about, never noticed. She hid her real self.

He flipped over and looked above at Great White Death's jaws clamping open and closed, but sideways on the edge two feet above them. Blood and body matter dripped out of the mouth, off the wretched teeth, and onto Lex's face.

Five minutes. Maybe less, then he could move again.

The teeth moved forward above him somehow, like the shark wiggled up the smooth rock, and then there he was, his very eye open and staring down at them. At him, at Lex. That one dark eye, in swirling madness of black, got a really good look at him, and the beast's mouth slowly, slowly closed.

Lex's couldn't breathe until Great White Death did. He could outlast him.

His life purpose was clear to him now.

A new way of balance, not the hunt.

His lungs screamed for air. He had more sweat than rainwater on his flesh, and more blood than sweat, it seemed. They measured each other up, two killers wanting now to kill each other.

Lex held his breath.

The great shark rolled his eye back, and swiftly slipped away from Lex's sight, and he heard a splash as he went back under to breathe.

Now, Lex thought. He inhaled, gasped.

He scooped Melody up and ran, ran, ran, calling out for Diane, hoping she'd wake up and help keep Melody alive.

He'd done it. It was possible, and it was amazing. Still, Lex felt wary mixed with the ecstasy.

… That eye. He couldn't stop seeing it as he ran through the windy, pelting rain. That was a wicked, wicked eye. It was on *him*.

CHAPTER 8 – DAY 5

Diane watched as Lex wiped Melody's white brow of sweat. It came right back. All the blood vessels in her best friend's eyes had burst in the attack, and those sultry eyes were now completely red with but a hint of black in the middles that rapidly fluctuated in size as her dazed eyes roamed without direction.

It had been an hour since Lex brought Melody back, leg and foot gone, flesh gnarled and turning black at the edges as Joseph went to work trying to stop the bleeding. The back of her head was a bloody pulp, and Lex said the giant shark had dragged her on her back in a head-swinging motion. Melody hadn't yet spoken.

Diane swallowed the fear and tears. She hardened inside, deciding not to feel as she watched Lex gaze down into Melody's feverish face with compassion and...adoration?

Was Lex really cracking up? His hands shook, and it didn't pass by Diane how Lex had tears streaming down his face when he came in screaming for Diane. All his shark legends, all his intensive studies... Could the reality of being trapped by a killer great white shark be breaking some delicate hold Lex had between his obsession with sharks and sanity?

The story was that the two of them went out to break the champagne cooler. They couldn't see. They got too close to the water, and the shark attacked. Lex saved her life from the monster's jaws.

Diane wished more than anything that Melody would regain consciousness and talk. She didn't like it, but her gut pulled her in a direction that confused and infuriated her. Lex was off. Diane wanted to hear what Melody had to say.

They all sat around her by the rekindled fire, not talking, just waiting.

*

Marty Hammerstein had never liked Lex, nor did he see what Diane saw in him. Too many students, too many research trips. He could tell the bad fruit, but not why it spoiled or where.

Looking at Melody was devastating to him. Part of him wished the damn shark had finished it fast so she wouldn't be suffering like this. She was good fruit, and brilliant. Kind, even with her brash ways. Why her?

Like Diane, Marty watched Lex with Melody closely. Lex seemed manic and frenzied, as though it were Diane lying before him, dying in agony. Even though the fire had dried his and what was left of Melody's clothes, Lex was as covered in sweat as she was.

Marty didn't get close to students personally. That wasn't why he taught. He taught so he could research all his life. Still, Diane held a special place in his heart for her strength and wit. No, Marty didn't believe Lex's story. He never believed any of Lex's stories, but the things running through his mind as Lex murmured, "She has to make it. She has to. Please, Melody, hold on. You can, you can. I'm here," well, Marty wasn't used to this much speculation about a person's character.

Weird is what it was. Marty knew Lex was too cool. Was this the real Lex?

No, Marty thought. He put pieces together, but nothing really fit except outrageous imaginings and far-fetched what-could-bes about who Lex actually was, and those dark thoughts went to places that made Marty uncomfortable, yet enraged.

As time ticked by and Melody moaned, bright red eyes rolling back in her head now and again, Marty's patience wore each time Lex coaxed Melody. He talked to her like a lover. As if they'd been bosom buddies for twenties years, even, if not extreme affection.

Weird is what that was.

Marty stood up. "Lex," he said quietly. "You need a break. Come with me, come sit with the supplies, just for a spell."

Lex's head shot up at him. "I'm fine. It's Melody. We all should be focusing on making her well. Better. She has to live."

"Hey," Joseph said. "Maybe Dr. Hammerstein is right, Lex. I think we're all concerned about you."

"Me?" he said as he turned back to Melody and caressed her cheek. "Look at her."

Aaron, sitting next to Lex, put his hand on Lex's shoulder. "Man, I agree. Go. Go sit with Dr. Hammerstein. You've been through so much and you're in shock. Take a breather, Lex."

Lex's eyes bulged, and instantly his face turned stony, and then he looked across Melody's blood soaking through the bandages around the back of her head at Diane. "You'll keep it up? You'll take care of her. Talk to her. She'll hear you and fight." He looked up at Marty. "All right."

Marty settled on a net, and Lex plopped on the floor, hand tracing the curve of the point of the harpoon, avoiding eye-contact.

He'd wanted to get Lex alone and ask questions while he appeared in his shaken and unbalanced state, but now it was just Lex. A sadness about him, almost depression, but none of the anxiety and out-of-character behavior. That ticked Marty off, but he was going to ask his questions anyway. He would just be more careful with how he phrased things.

Anger flared up inside Marty as he watched Lex adopt that cool exterior. He wanted to stifle it or he'd speak brashly, but now, alone with him and away from the others, from watching Melody bleed in pain, he decided to take matters directly to the point.

"What really happened, Lex?"

Lex blinked at him. "I told you."

"No, Lex." Marty stared at him, pausing. Lex met his gaze with a challenge in his eyes, one Marty didn't like. "I know." He left it at that to see what Lex would do or say. Marty didn't *know* anything, but if Lex thought he did, became convinced of it, then truth would be revealed.

Lex's tone was soft and light. "You know a lot."

"I do."

Tension filled Marty's shoulders.

"Okay. I'll bite. You seem, I don't know, biased. What do you know?" Lex leaned forward and let go of the harpoon.

Marty took his time answering, trying to unnerve the kid. It wasn't working. Lex's eyes were friendly and guarded at the same time. "I know about you."

Again, Marty knew nothing, but he'd set the bait. What would Lex say next?

To Marty's surprise, Lex hung his head and put his hands in his thick, black curls. "I'm so weak. You can see it." Marty heard anguish in his voice. Sincere. Had he been wrong?

Still, Lex could be playing him. "I see more," he tested.

Lex, still gripping his hair, began banging the sides of his head and his ears in rapid bursts. "It was awful. Seeing it, trying to save her." Lex gazed up at Marty with tears in his eyes. "I've seen all three get eaten by that shark, and I... I think I'm cracking up. I blocked out Oliver, but Chas...and then, right there in my grasp, Melody being destroyed." His face paled, yet still he was covered in sweat. "Dr. Hammerstein, I think it's breaking me. It's breaking me up into little pieces of what I once felt as security."

"Security?"

"These things don't really happen. I don't know how I survived all three attacks, but I know luck has worn out."

"Why did you two go out at all? It's ridiculous." It was getting harder to stay stern. What if Marty sensed Lex being disturbed by it all and that was it? As far as he knew, that was the first time Lex admitted to being with Oliver when he was killed by the shark. Could be messing him up, and maybe what Marty always sensed in him as untrustworthy was actually a man on the edge.

"It was. It all is. Can't you see?"

"Yes."

Lex looked down again, and in a quiet voice, said, "Dr. Hammerstein, I want to kill it. We have guns." He looked at Marty with intent. "You and me can go out at daybreak and hunt him. I don't want to involve anyone else in case something happens. You've fought sharks. I've only studied them, but I know how to use guns better than anyone here."

"You do?" Marty raised his eyebrows.

"I was raised hunting. Dad was military. I know guns." His eyes begged. "Please. You and me, and everybody else stays here. After what he's done, we have to end him." Lex's eyes teared up again, but in rage. "I want to end him."

Marty still had a funny feeling, something he couldn't put his finger on. But, he too wanted to destroy that beast of hell. Marty knew Melody couldn't possibly make it without real medical care. The other kids all acted like they knew, but not Lex, and Marty knew Lex knew the truth deep down. "We could."

Lex's eyes reddened and his cheeks darkened. "Yes, you and I. You and I. I forget my grammar, Doc." No smile, nothing but fury.

It was infectious.

"Yes, okay, Lex. We stay up, we tell the others what we're going to do, and we do it." The uneasy feeling faded into a mission of revenge.

*

When Lex returned to Melody, the pain and joy both came with the sight of her. Beautiful, unique Melody. He had to make sure…but Dr. Hammerstein was talking to the others of their plan to shoot up Great White Death tomorrow.

Dr. Hammerstein was too good. Insightful. But too good-hearted, wanting to believe the best in everyone. It wasn't hard for Lex to keep up the freaked-out-by-shark-death act and incite Hammerstein to go shark shooting. Dr. Hammerstein wanted to believe everybody had his values.

Lex didn't want to *know* Dr. Hammerstein, and he wasn't taking a chance with the shark again until Diane. Dr. Hammerstein had let Lex down. Lex thought the man liked him, but now he knew Dr. Hammerstein had never thought well of him.

Great White Death knew Lex, wanted him most of all. Lex could feel the shark's blood lust for him like the rain covered him each time he went outside.

Bunny sat where he had been before talking to Dr. Hammerstein. Diane was asleep, holding Melody's cramped hand.

Upon hearing the killing plan, Aaron and Joseph wanted to go with them, but Dr. Hammerstein said too many targets would damage their chances.

Lex wanted Bunny to move, but he said nothing and sat behind Diane, stroking her arm, watching Melody. She had to, had to live! He was covering beautifully with the crazy shark obsessive act, having seen such awful things, and once Dr. Hammerstein and the guys stopped talking, they fell asleep one by one. At last, as Dr. Hammerstein closed his eyes, he said, "Lex, sleep. You need rest for tomorrow."

The idea of taking his eyes off Melody again was unbearable, but he could at least fake it. He hoped so very much, but he knew he might wake, and Melody would be gone. Only he would know her, the real her.

He stretched out behind Diane and thought about the wonderful things that made up Melody.

It had to be before dawn, but the sky was, of course, pitch black with the storm covering any possible sunrise. Lex hammed up the act and lightly snored. He listened to Melody's breathing grow more and more rapid. He didn't want it to end this way, but he saw. He saw.

"Yes, Melody, yes. You're doing just fine. Now, breathe for me." Bunny's gentle, soft voice had been at it with Melody for hours. That made Lex happy. Bunny was taking good care of Melody, and maybe he should rest. He could tell it was near the end for Melody, and his heart was dying. He would sleep through it, deal with it tomorrow when he took Dr. Hammerstein out to hunt Great White Death, shoot him in the back, and sink him in the sea.

Then, off to a sweet slumber Lex went, hand on Diane's hip.

*

Like Lex, Bunny knew Melody's death would be any time. Bunny wouldn't let her go alone. She held her hand, wiped sweat and blood from her, and now that the sky had lightened enough to say it was daytime again, Melody moaned more, eyes rolling, and Bunny made out some words.

Melody might have a moment of clarity before her time. Bunny leaned over her face and gently kissed her cheek.

Instantly, Melody's red eyes rolled over and looked directly at Bunny. Right in the eyes. There! There was Melody.

"Oh my God!" Bunny gasped. "Melody, can you hear me?" Was it possible she might make it?

Melody's mouth moved. Rasping came out.

"What? Try again. Come on. You can do it." Bunny could tell Melody had something to tell her. It was the intensity of her bright red eyes, and those dilating pupils steadied on Bunny.

"Water."

"Yeah, here, here," Bunny whispered, and held a thermos of water to Melody's lips. Melody grabbed it and swallowed, swallowed until it was all gone. Some liquid leaked out of the back of the base of her head and she sighed. Then she looked back at Bunny, her breathing heavy. "I have to tell you."

"What? What is it?" Bunny wanted to tell her to stop, rest, tell her later, but there was a feeling to Melody's intensity, and Bunny had to adhere to Melody's wishes. It might keep her going.

"Lies. Lex lies." She lifted her head, wincing at the pain. "He…"

Her words fell away to a horrid coughing fit and blood shot out of her mouth onto her chest.

"What, Melody? He what?" Bunny leaned her ear close to Melody's lips. "Take it easy. Whisper it."

"Lex pushed. Lex pushed me into the shark's teeth." She heaved in, and blood dripped out of the side of her mouth.

"He saved you."

"He pushed…me. In." Melody sat straight up and grabbed Bunny's long hair, pulling her up to her face. "Lex is a killer. Killer."

Bunny gasped as Melody fell back, eyes rolled up forever in her head, and one last burst of breath left her.

Dead.

Bunny sat stunned for several moments, and then looked around. She carefully leaned over Diane to peer at Lex, fearing that he'd heard Melody's last words.

He was out with a spot of drool on the floor under his mouth.

Bunny looked around some more, eyes landing on the salvage from the yacht. She quickly made a plan, and immediately executed it. She knew in her heart and soul that

Melody was right, that this was the thing Bunny sensed about Lex. Not much escaped Bunny, but she never could figure out what vibe it was Lex had that made her not want to be, well, now that she knew, a target.

Bunny was shy, yes, but she watched. Shy, but tough from a long life of being put down by her family, manipulative men, and jealous girls.

She flew into action.

CHAPTER 9 – DAY 6

Diane woke first out of that same nightmare of her as the last shark and being eaten back to front. She quickly turned to Melody, remembering the pain and horror.

Melody was dead. "No!" Diane wailed, and threw her arms around cold Melody's body, waking everybody up.

Mass confusion and grief ensued among them all, and Lex, upon seeing Melody's body, cried out, covered his face, and stormed out of the keep, rubbing his wet eyes.

Joseph stayed the toughest, and comforted both sobbing Diane and Aaron until Dr. Hammerstein, between heaving breaths, obviously trying to stay strong, said, "Bunny. Bunny's not here. Where's Bunny?"

Diane lifted herself off her friend's corpse and looked around. Bunny had been at Melody's head. She wiped her eyes. "Bunny?" she called out.

"Look," Joseph said. "D, look. The harpoon is gone. I mean, the huge, can't miss it harpoon." He sounded baffled.

"Bunny," Diane said. "Bunny left, and she took the harpoon."

"Did she go to kill the shark?" Aaron asked.

"Dunno," Diane murmured.

"We have to see what else is missing," Dr. Hammerstein said, "And look for her."

"No," Joseph told him. "If Bunny left us and took that, we'll never find her."

"On this tiny island? Of course, we will," Aaron said.

"No," said Joseph. "Bunny was raised in the country in Idaho, lived on the land when she was a kid."

"She did?" Diane asked him, cocking her head.

"Yeah. Her parents made her and her six siblings work for them until they inherited some money and built a cabin. She climbed her way out of that."

"How do you know so much about her? She never talks," Diane said.

Joseph gave Diane a small smile. "She's shy. You have to ask her questions. But if Bunny wants to hide out with that harpoon, none of us have the skills to find her, even on this tiny island. She'll use the storm to her advantage."

Diane looked at Melody's shell one last time and said, "But, why?"

Nobody had an answer, and Diane broke the silence with, "We have to bury Melody." Her voice cracked, but she pulled it back together. "Dr. Hammerstein, your and Lex's plan can wait a few hours. I'll get Melody's phone, turn it on, see if we have anything."

Thunder crashed.

"Or not," Aaron told her. "No way today is different than yesterday."

Still, Diane got Melody's cell phone from her blanket palette from the night before and tried it. "Nothing. Nothing!" She turned it off.

Diane fisted her hands. "Lex," she hissed.

"I know, right?" said Joseph. "D, is he losing it? Like he said, shark thing?"

"He admitted he was with Oliver when the shark got him to me last night," Dr. Hammerstein said. "He said he'd blocked it out, that it all was too much, that he was weak."

Diane sighed and rubbed her face. "I just don't get it."

Dr. Hammerstein put his arm around Diane's shoulders. "I'm with Diane. Let's bury poor Melody. We'll find Lex outside, and he'll help."

"There's nowhere to bury. It's all rock," said Joseph. "Except for the sea lion beach, and nobody wants to get close to that."

Diane, still not looking at Melody ever again when she was like that, like she'd been ripped up and was just a pile of meat and bones, said, "We'll weigh her with rocks and sink her. We have to do it."

And that's what they did. Diane directed them, but she kept her eyes off Melody's destroyed body. A suspicion rose in her. When she'd first seen Melody dead, her head was tossed back and red eyes rolled up in her head. Her mouth had been open with blood dried down one side of her chin.

Had she said something to Bunny that made Bunny leave?

Diane glanced at Lex as he tossed her friend's body over the edge where the yacht had been, and dashed back to them where they waited, standing far from the water's edge.

As crazy as Lex had become over the killings, he wasn't too crazy to be the one to get close to the water to bury Melody despite his multiple mind-breaking experiences with the killer shark. Diane noted this and put it in the back of her mind. Melody dying was making her as crazy as Lex.

As soon as he reached them, he put his hand on Dr. Hammerstein's shoulder. "We go. We go now." He gestured at the rest of them. "You all, back to the keep and stay there no matter what. Diane." He looked her deep in the eyes. "I promise I'll make it right."

She nodded. She didn't smile at him. She might not ever smile again.

CHAPTER 10

Aaron didn't make eye-contact with Joseph or Diane as the three of them sat around the fire after Dr. Hammerstein and Lex left. The other two talked in hushed tones, as if anyone could hear them, about Lex. Lex, this. Lex, that.

Aaron never thought of himself as brave. He was big, and people equated that with being tough. 6'3" goes a long way when it came to seeming intimidating.

Right then, as he listened to Diane's voice waver as she said Melody's name, and suspicions that she'd told Bunny something about Lex, making her leave, Aaron knew he had to take action. For real. Be 6'3" in attitude like he got in respect.

As Joseph speculated this idea of Diane's with noncommittal phrases, Aaron interrupted with, "We all know it. Lex. We all three know." He looked up at Joseph. "You have always known." He turned to Diane's worried, tired eyes. "You now know."

"What?" Diane said. "What do you know? That Lex is a maniac? Is that what you both know?" She looked at Joseph, who tilted his head to the side, eyebrows pushing together. "He's somehow killed three people, like Melody saw Chas, with a 400-year-old cursed shark? And now, he's getting it to kill our teacher?" Her tone was flat. No fear, no anger. Defeat.

Aaron looked down, and heard Joseph whisper, "Yeah, D. I think that's it."

He looked back up. "Okay, you guys. I'm going to stop him. I'm going to stop it from happening."

Diane stared at him, eyes wide. "With what? The guns are gone."

Aaron punched his palm. "I know how to be sneaky."

Joseph stood up with Aaron. "No, no. You can't go alone."

Aaron waved his hand between Joseph and Diane as she, too, stood, looking up at him, concerned. "One of us has to stop Lex from... Not all three of us. He'll notice all three. I'll go, and you two, leave in about 20 minutes, come after me. I'm betting they're at the beach."

"What makes you say that?" said Joseph.

Aaron shook his head. "Because that's the easiest place to find that damn shark." He looked at them. "I don't know why he's doing this...do either of you...? Diane, do you have any idea?"

She frowned and looked at the ground. "No. I feel stupid. But no."

"Don't feel stupid," said Joseph. "I had no clue until our talk now. I never would guess Lex could, well, murder people. I mean, has that been a long-term plan for him? Studying sharks all his life so he could kill all the people closest to him with one? How does that even work? Getting a shark to kill people?"

"But," Diane said, "Aaron said you knew."

Joseph shook his head, looking at the floorboards. "I mean, I knew something was different, I guess."

Aaron put his hand on Diane's shoulder. "Let's stop speculating. Action. It's time for action."

She slowly raised her eyes to his. Intense stare, inscrutable. Her chin stayed tucked down. "Okay. Okay."

*

Lex shot Dr. Hammerstein dead in the back of the head the second the teach looked south, away from him, and they were closest they'd get to water. Lex didn't think twice. He'd patiently waited. No time to know Dr. Hammerstein, and his disappointment was so great in the man, that the knowing wouldn't be worth the risk.

Besides, no bat body.

Lex tightened his hood over his head, lifted the professor's booted ankles, and began dragging him across the sea lion beach to the shoreline. Yes, it made him nervous—his heart pounded like a rave tent—but the time crunch distracted him. Risk was necessary now.

If Joseph talked Diane into thinking the worst of Lex, what would happen after the knowing? She would leave him for sure. Then, what about his happy life ahead of him, the greatest thing he'd ever wished for?

His feet were washed with rough waves before he knew it. The storm was so thick that he didn't know he'd reached the water's edge until he stood in the sea.

Okay, he thought, *just swing him around into the water, get his gun, throw that big rock on him, and get the hell out. Fast as possible.*

Lex heaved on the body, and the dead professor swooshed through frothy waves. Lex was pleased that the gun simply floated out of his clamped hand once buoyant. He scooped it up and stuck it in his waistband.

He sloshed through the waves to get the nearby rock that was to hold Hammerstein under the surface so that nobody would find him. He reached it and bent at the knees for the heavy chunk of solid earth.

Just then, he felt a heavy wave current coming at him, bigger and stronger than the usual storm waves, and he knew.

Great White Death. He caused that flush of water. *Oh, crap,* he thought, and knew better than to spin around to see him.

Lex hopped the waves, hit the gravel beach, and made a run for it, but…

"Stop!" A palm slammed onto Lex's chest out of nowhere. Lex groaned, and made Aaron's face out through the heavy rainfall.

"Aaron, man, the shark. The damn shark!"

"I saw it. I saw you shoot him, Lex."

No time, he thought. He peeked over his shoulder but couldn't make out the shoreline from where he was. But the sea lions…they squealed, several of them, when they'd been huddled in groups waiting it out.

Lex looked back at Aaron. He could make out his expression of anger, pain, confusion.

Confusion was a weakness Lex could exploit.

"I was aiming for the shark. Man, I'm telling you. Let's go, come on!" He tried to get out of Aaron's iron grip.

"No, no. You can't tell me I didn't see and hear what I saw and heard. You dragged him to the water!"

"Yeah, I shot, but it was an accident to hit Hammerstein."

"Hammerstein? Dr. Hammerstein, you mean? No, Lex." He yelled to be heard. "You shot him dead in the head. The back of the head."

How could Aaron even have seen that?

Just then, Lex's fear hit them both, but like them, Great White Death couldn't navigate well in the dastardly storm. He rammed Lex in the back with his head, and Lex and Aaron were flung inward on the beach.

Lex's survival instincts kicked in. He pressed—hard—on the nerves in the insides of Aaron's thumbs, squirming on top of Aaron, and the guy loosened his grip on Lex's arms, and Aaron yelped and let go, writhing underneath him.

Lex used the lubrication and lightness of seawater to slide around and under Aaron and put Aaron on top of him.

"No, man, no!"

Lex saw Aaron put his hands out, palms forward and fingers spread, and Lex knew he saw the killer shark of legend, coming right for him.

The screaming started before Aaron's legs burst into bright red blood, and Lex made out the shark's mouth and face, teeth gnawing on Aaron's legs, almost gently, yet with a vicious coldness of method. His eyes were open and black and looking…right at Lex.

Great White Death effortlessly chewed up Aaron's legs to his hips as Aaron mindlessly slapped the thing's blood-smattered snout, and Lex was soaked in rain, seawater, and now Aaron's ever-flowing blood.

The knowing came, without warning to Lex, as Aaron screeched and babbled in short, piercing bursts as the shark hit those tender spots that make every man squeal his essence.

None of the others see the angels like I do… I see green and pink… If the days end as written I will fall…

Lex's eyes rolled back in his head as the shark savored Aaron's flesh and screams, Aaron's blood flying as the rain, and thunder, lightning took over the world. Lex, covered in the blood and pieces of flesh and bone, thankfully not his, was paralyzed, in ecstasy.

Mindful, be mindful... Mama wouldn't have liked this... She would have spanked, and the hurt ones go on forgetting everything... As the ice melts, so do the ancient lie...

Aaron, Lex thought, *this man, this great friend.* Lex had no idea of his ancient soul. No idea the things Aaron had been through and knew. Now, Lex knew them too, and he would have done anything to keep Aaron from dying just then, but Great White Death had done the fatal damage, and with a slow, guttural groan, what was left of Aaron fell in pieces on and over Lex as the shark chomped his whole body up and let pieces of wonderful, blessed Aaron gush out of his maw.

Half of Aaron's head, the top half, landed next to Lex's face with a salty, bloody splash. He opened his eyes all the way and stared at Aaron's empty eye sockets.

Lex gasped and instantly was on his feet, wiping water and massive amounts of blood from his face, heart pounding with the thrill of the *knowing* and the terror of standing face-to-face with the killer great white monster.

Lex hopped back and fell over a sea lion. Great White Death lunged, but missed Lex, instead, impaling the sea lion.

The shark ran out of breath then, it seemed to Lex, because he finished the sea lion off in just a few gruesome and intestine gushing snaps of his teeth, and quickly slid back into the sea.

Lex jumped up, turned, and ran for his life in the opposite direction of the sea.

CHAPTER 11

"You can cry."

"Joseph. Really?"

Diane rolled her eyes as she and Joseph put out the fire in the fire pit.

He smiled at her. She shook her head and threw a chair seat on top of the smoldering ashes. "You know I'll cry about it when this is all over. Right now, just staying focused. Not thinking."

"Have you ever done that? Not think?" He cocked his head at her.

She wiped sweat from her face, eyed him. "Right now, I am thinking of what the fuck!"

"Yeah." He'd been trying to lighten the mood, Diane knew, and she felt bad that she'd been snappy. His voice deepened at that last word. Men always felt bad when they didn't fix the woman's problems. She knew this, but Lex never seemed to be like that.

No, Lex had never been a regular guy one bit. That's what kept her interest—he was so very different. Now, she had to face just how different he really was.

Half of her couldn't accept it. It was all a line of coincidences. Misunderstandings. Lex had been in the wrong place at the wrong time...three times... His obsession with shark lore made those coincidental times crack his mind, his self-contained, stands-alone mind.

"You're okay," Joseph said, and put his arm around her shoulders. She stiffened.

"What?"

"D, do you even know what just happened?"

Diane realized she looked up at Joseph. She laid on the wood floor, and he was pulling her into sitting position. "What…what happened?"

"You just fell. Boom. You were still for a minute like you were thinking about something really bad, and then—I caught you, though. You didn't hit your head." He furrowed his brow. "Are you okay? D?"

"Yeah, yeah." Oh God, she hadn't fallen out like that since ninth grade in geometry class during a presentation. The thing with narcolepsy was that she'd learned such coping mechanisms that she stopped passing out altogether long ago, but great stress or shock could still do it.

Joseph kept his arm around her and pulled a water bottle out of his coat. "Here, drink."

She did, and although she hadn't been thirsty, the pure, good water disappeared in 10 seconds.

She realized she was seeing in color again.

Oh, that one must have been a doozy, she thought. She hadn't woken colorblind since her dog got hit by a car and killed in seventh grade while she watched.

"What was that, Diane?"

"It's…like my power naps when I can't help it and fall asleep. Sometimes stress…"

"D, this is the most stressful it can get, I think."

"I think you're right," she said, putting her face in her cold hands. Sweating and cold.

"Do you need food? Look, why don't you let me go after Aaron? You stay here."

She snapped her head over to him. "No. No, I'm going. I have to see."

Joseph was quiet a moment, then said, "What do you have to see?" His voice had an edge of darkness and despair, as though he could foretell the future, and saw how very dark it was going to get. It gave Diane another chill.

"I have to see Lex. I have to hear it from him."

Thunder so loud it shook the lighthouse keeper's home stopped conversation for a few seconds.

Diane stood up. She felt wired, wide awake.

Joseph stood with her and dropped the arm he'd had around her shoulders.

"We go. Now." Diane didn't look back at Joseph as she went for the door, choosing to leave safety in the name of finding out and knowing the truth for herself.

*

Joseph hated this, all of it. Yes, he loved Diane and had since he laid eyes on her, and for six months loathed thinking of those two, Diane and Lex, together. Her loving gazes at him, her talking about things that were so wonderful about him.

Joseph had a way of knowing someone's character on meeting him. When he first laid eyes on Lex, he thought of a person filled with his own shadow.

Now, that made sense. It hadn't at the time, and over the years getting to know Lex, the first impression faded, but had reared its ugly head when Diane and Lex got close.

He thought it was his broken heart still hoping, but he'd never, ever hope for this to be the way it ended.

Lex was smart; Joseph knew it. He also knew that, because Lex was brilliant, they all might never come back from this tiny rock of an island. Joseph set his mind on making sure that didn't happen.

He and Diane walked side-by-side through the raging storm. It was so dark it might have been dusk instead of morning. They didn't speak; it was hard enough to figure out what was right in front of them with this strong rain, and they'd have to yell to be heard over the thunder and wind. No doing that lest they be heard before they found Lex.

"I think this is the edge of the sea lion beach," Diane called into Joseph's ear. "Can you see anything?"

He shook his head, holding his hand over his eyes to no real effect. "Let's hang here and watch, listen."

They did. Joseph could have sworn he heard splashing, not just rough water on the beach, but splashing, and then he heard a sea lion squeal.

Down the beach on the right, the gray wall held a bright red spot of spraying blood for a flash of a moment.

In Joseph's mind's eye, the red lingered, an omen. He shivered, and took Diane's hand, not thinking. She didn't let go.

"Oh my God," she said.

"You saw that?"

"Yeah. Hell yeah." Her usually pale face was as white as snow in the constant lightning.

Out of the haze of nothing, a man's form came dashing toward them. Joseph pulled Diane backward.

"Hey, hey!" It was Lex, and he was just upon them. He waved a gun in one hand, and had another tucked in the front of his waistband.

Joseph put his free hand out. "Stop, Lex." He cleared his throat, unheard, because Lex kept coming. "Stop!"

Lex slowed to a walk, holding out his hands after sticking the gun he'd held in the back of his pants. He waved his palms. "We have to run, run!"

"What?" Diane yelled. "What happened? What is going on? Where's Aaron, Lex? Dr. Hammerstein?" She squinted her eyes at him, tilted her head, and let go of Joseph's hand. She folded her arms across her chest.

"No time!" Lex stopped in front of Diane, glanced at Joseph, then back to Diane.

Joseph saw the annoyance in Lex's simple look at him. Why would Lex be annoyed?

It was all true. It was. Joseph knew it now.

Diane saw it but wasn't acknowledging it.

"Look," Lex said to her, "we have to run."

"No, you explain this madness to me. Now!" She hit him in the chest. "Are you a fucking murderer?" Her face was now flushed red with fury. Joseph had never seen her angry.

Desperation filled Lex's eyes. Joseph was surprised. It had to be genuine. As crazy as Lex was turning out to be, was he capable of actually loving Diane?

"Did he tell you this?" Lex gestured at Joseph without looking at him. "Who? Diane, you know me. Better than anyone. I'll explain, but…"

"But what?"

"Look, here." He took the guns out of his waistband and handed them to Joseph, who gripped them tightly at his sides by the triggers.

"I can show you," said Lex, "but just you, Diane. It's you, of all people in the world, who knows the real me. I want to know you like that. You're a sea deeper than any ocean, full of complexities and great goodness."

"What are you talking about?" Her eyes looked saddened like Lex's.

A great, hard gust of wind and rain suddenly obscured Joseph's view of them, and he felt a sharp tug on his shoulder. He stumbled backward several steps, trying to keep his balance.

"What the—?"

A dainty hand covered his mouth.

Bunny.

She said into his left ear, "Shh. Come here, with me, come back here."

"But, Diane. She's not safe, she's with him," he said after she slowly removed her hand. He looked over his shoulder at her. She was a mess, having been in the rough for…how long? It couldn't be just hours, could it?

"We'll get him, come." Her sharp eyes told him the red cloud of blood he'd seen hovering was an omen that didn't have to come true just then.

CHAPTER 12

"Don't worry about him," Lex told Diane. Joseph had simply disappeared without either of them noticing, and Diane was freaking out.

"But…what could have happened to him? Lex, you are standing right here. What the hell!" She swung her drenched head back and forth.

"I think he took off, to be honest."

"Why?"

Lex had to get her mind off Joseph. He could feel it…this was it. The greatest knowing of his lifetime was at hand. He just had to get Diane to the water, to trusting him to go to the water.

"Because, Diane, he's always loved you. You know it. Don't deny it. He filled your head with lies about me. They all did. It's jealousy. Fear. This shark. It's driving us all mad!" He knew he sounded convincing. Diane's face showed uncertainty.

"You, Diane, know me. Come on." He cupped her face in his wet, cold hands, and her eyes softened. "You know."

He kissed both of her cheeks. She didn't pull away and closed her eyes.

"I want to show you something. It's about Aaron and Dr. Hammerstein. Don't worry, it's safe. We're hunting the shark. Down by the water."

"Then, what was that seal about? The one who screamed, and all that blood?"

Lex shifted, and put his hands on her shoulders. "That was another shark. We killed it. Come, I'll show you. It's safe."

Diane took a step toward the inlet. "Wait." She stopped. "You guys have no guns. You just gave them to Joseph."

"You think those guns touched the shark? No. No way. We found Bunny's harpoon. That's what we're hunting with." He delivered it all with powerful energy, and he knew she believed him. "Diane, please. It's me."

Her blue eyes turned into balls of newborn suns. "You better not be fucking with me, Lex." She said it with such dead calm that Lex felt a pang through his heart at the pain she was about to be put through. How could he do that to her? Yes, he could mastermind this into the ground when she lived to tell…and make her love him, be with him. He was that good at people. Hurting her to the brink of her being was the cruelest thing he could do to the person he loved most in the world.

His shoulders slumped as those burning blue suns sabotaged him with a newfound sensitivity…not quite a conscience. He stared down at the sluggy, rocky water swirling around his boots. No, he couldn't do it to her. He simply couldn't.

"Lex. Look at me."

He turned his face up, slowly raising his eyes to hers. He let her see his true self through his eyes, the way he did with cats and dogs, making them run or snap at him, and she no longer burned with fury of creative righteousness. She was sad, scared, and tired.

"Let's go. Let's go back to the lighthouse keep. Forget it all, and wait for the phone to get signal," she said, and walked closer to him. He kept penetrating her being with his damaged and swollen soul, filled with dozens of other souls, and each and every kill, he spilled from him memory into her eyes. Her blue irises turned hues bright, baby blue with the rush of the knowing, gray with his memories of loss at the end of adored human lives, then hazel, pale green with each soul Lex carried now shared with her. He knew she got it, all of it, and he fell into her open arms, sobbing openly, not caring, not a single sense of his very humility, being stripped naked of his self-worth, of his everything, before Diane.

She didn't grasp him back, but he knew the psychic connection he'd linked with her had been as intense for her as for him. It would take a stunned minute.

"Yes, Lex, let's go," Diane said in his ear, tucked under her chin. His tears made the breast of her beige soaked jacket even more discolored somehow. He realized his face must have been covered in blood and sea dirt. He raised his eyes to her.

Was she saying…what he thought she was saying? To go…to the shark? "You…want this too?" He told her, astounded. "You want what we can have?"

She put both gloved hands on either side of his face, a line creasing between her fine eyebrows. "Yes, come. Come on, let's do this. Let's go."

Lex clamped his hands on her forearms. He didn't know this kind of connection existed outside of the knowing. Diane, the only woman he's ever felt love for, tenderness with, took everything of him in her own way of knowing—through the depth of their love, and now wanted to sacrifice the pain for him to know her.

He grabbed her by the tops of her arms as his heartbeat pounded his head to a haze of glory. "Diane, I love you. I love you so much, I would anyway, but now, now…" He could see an eternity of fantastic connection and knowing in her eyes, her offering to him the same in return. She was telling him to take her to Great White Death. He heard her loud and clear.

"You... I have no words." He gasped, wiped his face, and then swung her around in front of him and shoved her stiff body toward the wall of storm at the sea line.

"No, no! Lex, what?" she screamed.

He knew it was going to be hard, hard for both of them for her to suffer this excruciating pair and fear, and this was her human being part of her crying. Her soul already spoke to him. "Soon, Diane, soon!"

He scooped her up in his arms, she'd begun to fight so hard, so he could contain her in a tight ball against his chest and abs, and rushed her to the water's edge while screaming for the shark to come.

Great White Death didn't disappoint, as though he now thought of Lex as a snack delivery service that would finish off his appetite if he was unsettled when through with offerings. His enormous, jagged fin rose from the water to signal the shark's anticipation, and as soon as Lex's boots rattled the ground closer in the water, waves around his thighs, the fin shot straight for him like a notched arrow flying, aiming in between the narrow walls of the rock beach.

Lex dropped Diane, flipped her over, kicked her legs out from under her. The excitement, and the moment of the moment was a divinity of excellence. Yes, Diane looked horrified, but that was the person, Diane. The soul Diane said this was it; this was her offering back to him.

Great White Death's disgusting and now-familiar face, along with snarled-back skin around his jagged and sharp teeth, zoomed toward Diane's ankles trailing in the water behind her...she stared up at Lex, eyes blank, and then—she closed her eyes and sunk like a rock. Her limps hands slip from his shocked grasp.

Fuck.

She fell out.

When Diane fell out like this, she was the same exact thing as dead weight to Lex.

He looked up at the gaping mouth, with a toothy chin that dragged the top of Diane's legs and back, all the way up... Great White Death wanted his food moving, desperately, if possible. Lex fell back into the water and tried to go low under the waves like she had, but it was no use. The shark snagged Lex in a full, tight and unendurably painful clamp on and through his knees, pulled him right out of the water, and shook him back and forth through the air like a cat might with a chipmunk snack. Spikes of agonizing pain ripped through his legs and nerves, up into his brain, and then the teeth snip, snip, snipped their way up to his buttocks, and impaled him there straight through, and that is when his brain cracked, and time stayed there, the great white shark's murderous teeth would forever crawl up his spine as he, himself, and his very essence came out of his mouth for both him and the shark to know. Lex didn't want to know this, never had he wanted to, but now, as the shark destroyed both his legs and worked on his middle, Lex knew he now deserved and would spend an eternity in teeth and madness.

EPILOGUE

"So, you say this woman Bunny killed the damn thing? Or the sleeper?" said Paul Blank, dropping a buck in the glass carafe with a post-it reading, "TIPS 4 STACI." He took his beer mug and shook his 60-year-old hairless head, eyeing Staci on the loaded side of the bar. "Hun, they saying these kids from the school killed the Great White Death, you hear 'em?"

Staci smiled at Paul Blank, squeezed his hand. "I told you. A woman brought him, a woman would put him back."

"Was she a witch?" asked Buddha from the end of the seafaring bar on the California pier.

"Nah," said the stranger next to Paul Blank. He was a young one, claimed to have helped the survivor. "And Bunny didn't make it. Only one survived."

"You said that. That's where you ended it," Paul Blank pointed out, three times excited, annoyed, and happy drunk. "So, when the shark crazy dude was chewed up by GWD, the fairy outlaw chick jumps him with the harpoon, but the girl don't wake up 'cuz she has sleeping-all-the-time problems."

"Right," said the stranger. "And the good man in love with her, he went in to get her when the techie Bunny harpooned the shark. He slid in that water fast. I saw it, that Bunny's shot stabbed sideways right through both eyes directly, and the shark still lived."

"That's some shit," said Staci. "How old did you say the two were?"

"Yeah," said Buddha, "and what's your name? I seen you before, but you keep to yourself."

"Lamar," he said, nodding his head at Buddha and dropping a dollar in Staci's tip jar as she handed him a refill on his draft beer. "I'm the lighthouse keeper on Aña Nuevo, come back once every few months to town for supplies. My brothers take the other 2/3rds of the year. This is my season."

"No keeper on 'at," Paul Blank pointed out, finger waving around Lamar.

"We have an agreement with the military," he said, pulling his black ballcap low over his black eyes. Paul Blank found him most fascinating, couldn't believe what he was hearing.

"The guy was 25, and the girl was 24, in this case. Pretty normal, huh?" said Lamar. He grinned at Paul, winked at Staci.

"I remember you now, yeah. Lamar Sutton. Your whole family has been with that island for, what? For-fucking-ever?"

Paul Blank shushed his hun, and said to Lamar, "So, the guy saving her, how did he get it?"

Lamar glanced around as though somebody who shouldn't hear anymore might have sneaked in the shabby shack of a bar, and then looked into his beer. "He got young Diana out of the waters, pushed her, all passed out, up on shore, and damn, that shark snatched him up while he took in some breath. He screamed, that poor young man. He cried for Diana and Bunny and Lex, that's how I figured out their names for sure.

"At this point, the harpoon went straight through GWD's head and he couldn't see. But he wasn't giving up. No."

"You seen this just two days ago? Because they woke you up?" Staci asked, and to Paul, she was slowing down the yarn.

"They took over my house in the storm, scared the crap outta me. First time I've seen GWD since three years ago when that same kid—Lex—came through listening to stories and I took him back to the island with me for a bit. He's charming, and you wouldn't believe how twisted his soul is. Everything I have seen and heard through those floorboards..." He looked around. "If any of you had any time with this shark, you know most of those legends are almost gospel. Right? You look in those round, black, sharp murderous eyes, you know all those tales are true."

"The guy Joseph died." Paul Blank leaned forward. "Staci, buy Lamar a shot of Crown on me." He smiled at her. "Thanks, honey."

"Thank you! It's just as much a treat to tell you all the shark is dead, dead, dead."

"So, what did the Bunny girl do? Assuming Diana is the one who beat the damn thing."

Lamar slammed the shot, wiped his mouth. It didn't get by Paul Blank that Staci watched and probably admired too much how casually the keeper held himself smooth and too cool for school for her benefit.

Paul Blank winked at his wife himself.

She rolled her eyes and grinned.

"Well," said Lamar, "it was rainy, so much rain! This was the best I could make out. Bunny, she jumps on the harpoon and rips it back out with her hands. I guess she thought that would unplug the shark, maybe. Then GWD didn't dip for a breath between deaths and ate her up, too." He looked all around, a pleased smile on his lips.

"Huh, wait, so how then did Diana do it?" said Buddha.

"She did. She got that harpoon out of the water, and bam! When GWD went under at last to breathe, she ran up the back of his tail and spine, then stabbed the harpoon through the top of his skull. I never heard a human make a sound like that which came out of this woman, Diana, when she vanquished the demon shark. It was like the voice of an unknown deity both being born and dying at the same time!"

"You are a poet, aren't you?" said Buddha.

"For 1/3rd of the year, I have books." He laughed. "But I have other plans now. Let me buy everybody a shot of Crown. You good?"

Shots were had, and Great White Death stories passed through the now-crowding room, despite the storm.

*

Lamar slipped out without even Paul Blank's eagle eye noticing. He turned the corner, tipped his slicker collar to the rain, and onward he made his way to the motel by the shore. He smiled to himself. He couldn't wait to tell them. They would love it.

Maybe not so much Diane. No, not yet. Not quite.

The One, though? He laughed aloud to the rainfall. He had this feeling, like his great-great-grandmother, the medicine woman of her time, had feelings, that they had a connection, a future.

Diane, or "Diana," as she chose to be called, what he felt about her was she would go even deeper in the studies than The One. He might know her for the rest of his life, too…

He reached the motel and pulled out his key, paused, and then held up his hand and knocked.

Diane opened the door, eyes and face pale, Bunny just behind her like a phantom shadow with long hair.

"You're back." A small slip of a smile crossed her lips and finished on Bunny's behind her.

"It's done." He went in and took off his wet coat, gloves, and boots. Sat on the bed across from the women. "Now, because you chose, I will tell you more. I will tell you the very tip of the basics we've been studying, and how what you two did has changed the way of the seas." He blinked and smiled, folding his hands. "You wanted to understand the sea? Well, you've left it all behind now, and all that's left are the oceans and their infinite existence."

 SEVERED**PRESS**

CHECK OUT OTHER GREAT DEEP SEA THRILLERS

THE BREACH
by Edward J. McFadden III

A Category 4 hurricane punched a quarter mile hole in Fire Island, exposing the Great South Bay to the ferocity of the Atlantic Ocean, and the current pulled something terrible through the new breach. A monstrosity of the past mixed with the present has been disturbed and it's found its way into the sheltered waters of Long Island's southern sea.

Nate Tanner lives in Stones Throw, Long Island. A disgraced SCPD detective lieutenant put out to pasture in the marine division because of his Navy background and experience with aquatic crime scenes, Tanner is assigned to hunt the creeper in the bay. But he and his team soon discover they're the ones being hunted.

INFESTATION
by William Meikle

It was supposed to be a simple mission. A suspected Russian spy boat is in trouble in Canadian waters. Investigate and report are the orders.

But when Captain John Banks and his squad arrive, it is to find an empty vessel, and a scene of bloody mayhem.

Soon they are in a fight for their lives, for there are things in the icy seas off Baffin Island, scuttling, hungry things with a taste for human flesh.

They are swarming. And they are growing.

"Scotland's best Horror writer" - Ginger Nuts of Horror

"The premier storyteller of our time." - Famous Monsters of Filmland

CHECK OUT OTHER GREAT
DEEP SEA THRILLERS

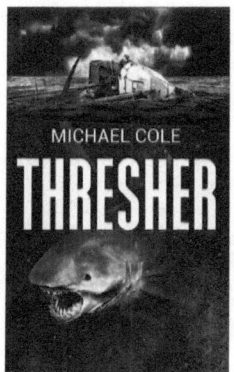

THRESHER
by Michael Cole

In the aftermath of a hurricane, a series of strange events plague the coastal waters off Florida. People go into the water and never return. Corpses of killer whales drift ashore, ravaged from enormous bite marks. A fishing trawler is found adrift, with a mysterious gash in its hull.

Transferred to the coastal town of Merit, police officer Leonard Riker uncovers the horrible reality of an enormous Thresher shark lurking off the coast. Forty feet in length, it has taken a territorial claim to the waters near the town harbor. Armed with three-inch teeth, a scythe-like caudal fin, and unmatched aggression, the beast seeks to kill anything sharing the waters.

THE GUILLOTINE
by Lucas Pederson

1,000 feet under the surface, Prehistoric Anthropologist, Ash Barrington, and his team are in the midst of a great archeological dig at the bottom of Lake Superior where they find a treasure trove of bones. Bones of dinosaurs that aren't supposed to be in this particular region. In their underwater facility, Infinity Moon, Ash and his team soon discover a series of underground tunnels. Upon exploring, they accidentally open an ice pocket, thawing the prehistoric creature trapped inside. Soon they are being attacked, the facility falling apart around them, by what Ash knows is a dunkleosteus and all those bones were from its prey. Now...Ash and his team are the prey and the creature will stop at nothing to get to them.

CHECK OUT OTHER GREAT DEEP SEA THRILLERS

SHARK: INFESTED WATERS
by P.K. Hawkins

For Simon, the trip was supposed to be a once in a lifetime gift: a journey to the Amazon River Basin, the land that he had dreamed about visiting since he was a child. His enthusiasm for the trip may be tempered by the poor conditions of the boat and their captain leading the tour, but most of the tourists think they can look the other way on it. Except things go wrong quickly. After a horrific accident, Simon and the other tourists find themselves trapped on a tiny island in the middle of the river. It's the rainy season, and the river is rising. The island is surrounded by hungry bull sharks that won't let them swim away. And worst of all, the sharks might not be the only blood-thirsty killers among them. It was supposed to be the trip of a lifetime. Instead, they'll be lucky if they make it out with their lives at all.

DARK WATERS
by Lucas Pederson

Jörmungandr is an ancient Norse sea monster. Thought to be purely a myth until a battleship is torn a part by one.

With his brother on that ship, former Navy Seal and deep-sea diver, Miles Raine, sets out on a personal vendetta against the creature and hopefully save his brother. Bringing with him his old Seal team, the Dagger Points, they embark on a mission that might very well be their last.

But what happens when the hunters become the hunted and the dark waters reveal more than a monster?

www.ingramcontent.com/pod-product-compliance
Lightning Source LLC
Chambersburg PA
CBHW051955170626
46808CB00007B/2637